THE NIGHT WORLD . . . .
LOVE HAS NEVER BEEN
SO DANGEROUS.

THE NIGHT WORLD isn't a place. It's all around us. The creatures of the Night World are beautiful and deadly and irresistible to humans. Your best friend could be one—so could your crush.

The laws of Night World are very clear: humans must never learn that Night World exists. And members of Night World must never fall in love with a human. Violate the laws and the consequences are terrifying. . . .

FOR MORE TALES FROM THE DARKNESS
BY L.J. SMITH, DON'T MISS:

Night World 1:
Secret Vampire, Daughters of Darkness, Spellbinder

Night World 2:
Dark Angel, The Chosen, Soulmate

Night World 3:
Huntress, Black Dawn, Witchlight

AND COMING SOON, THE DRAMATIC CONCLUSION:

Strange Fate

ALSO LOOK FOR:

Dark Visions:
The Strange Power, The Possessed, The Passion

NIGHT WORLD

The Ultimate Fan Guide

L.J. SMITH
AND ANNETTE POLLERT

SIMON PULSE
NEW YORK LONDON TORONTO SYDNEY

This book is a work of fiction. Any references to historical events, real people, or real locales are used fictitiously. Other names, characters, places, and incidents are the product of the author's imagination, and any resemblance to actual events or locales or persons, living or dead, is entirely coincidental.

SIMON PULSE

An imprint of Simon & Schuster Children's Publishing Division

1230 Avenue of the Americas, New York, NY 10020

First Simon Pulse paperback edition October 2009

Copyright © 2009 by Lisa J. Smith

All rights reserved, including the right of reproduction in whole or in part in any form.

SIMON PULSE and colophon are registered trademarks of Simon & Schuster, Inc.

NIGHT WORLD is a trademark of Lisa J. Smith.

For information about special discounts for bulk purchases, please contact Simon & Schuster Special Sales at 1-866-506-1949 or business@simonandschuster.com.

The Simon & Schuster Speakers Bureau can bring authors to your live event. For more information or to book an event contact the Simon & Schuster Speakers Bureau at 1-866-248-3049 or visit our website at www.simonspeakers.com.

Designed by Mike Rosamilia

The text of this book was set in Garamond 3.

Manufactured in the United States of America

10 9 8 7 6 5 4 3 2 1

Library of Congress Control Number 2009931428

ISBN 978-1-4424-0284-3

ISBN 978-1-4424-0285-0 (eBook)

For

Toni

—L. J. S.

For

Mom and Dad

—A. P.

→ Contents ←

Dear Readers,

It's hard to tell you how much the re-release of the Night World books means to me. It has allowed me to come full circle, to complete a cycle that began with *Secret Vampire*. It has allowed me to finish *Strange Fate*, which grew into an epic that included roles for almost every Night World character. And *Strange Fate* allowed me to show the origins of the Night World, the apocalypse that threatens to destroy it, and even a possible future in which the evil side of the Night World prevails.

I am often asked how I conceived the idea for the Night World series. It began when I wanted to write stand-alone novels that would combine horror and romance. But I wanted more: I wanted to do a series in which this Night World—a vast, secret world that exists within the everyday world—would slowly reveal itself to readers.

That's why the first book is called *Secret Vampire*: the inhabitants of the Night World, composed of vampires, shapeshifters, witches, and other supernatural creatures I wanted to invent, are hidden from humans. A vampire is necessarily a *secret* vampire . . . because of the laws.

I also wanted to write about a new kind of forbidden love. That's not easy—most good forbidden love topics were old by Shakespeare's time. But with this series, I could create the possibility of forbidden love simply by saying that the laws of the Night World prohibit a Night Person from falling in love with a human.

But I still needed one more ingredient. I needed the rise of the soulmate principle to actively force Night People to fall in love with humans, no matter how hard they fought against it. Voilà! Then it was just a matter of making up interesting characters and setting them loose in my head to see what they would do.

I often begin like that: sitting in a quiet room and searching for a sparkle in my mind that could become my new heroine. Sometimes it's easy and a whole character shimmers before me. Sometimes I only get the faintest firefly glimmer of a new girl, and I have to hold my breath and see if that glimmer will materialize into a three-dimensional person.

Heroes and anti-heroes are easier. It's just a matter of picking one that will be a true soulmate for my heroine. I have a whole collection of these characters in my mind, all trying to crash the party. And they're usually bad boys.

The settings and in-depth plot development are another layer of work. But often the characters just run off and do what they want, and I have trouble keeping up with their antics on my keyboard.

One thing I always do is look carefully at my characters and plot from all angles to make sure I'm not plagiarizing a book or series that I may have read before. That's just normal procedure for ethical authors: we make sure our stories aren't *too* much like another story we might have read. Of course, there are many ideas that have been around since the Babylonian myths, and many characters that are archetypal. But, really, it's almost impossible to take *many* things from the body of another author's work—say, someone else's character(s) or plot or story device—without actually intending to do so. I can't imagine wanting to do that. I wish I could say every author felt the same.

Poppy North is a character I examined very carefully. I wanted to make sure she wasn't too much like Bonnie McCullough, another petite character of mine from The Vampire Diaries. I didn't even want to plagiarize myself! But Poppy convinced me that she was a tough little squirt who by high school had already planned out her future, which is very unlike Bonnie. Poppy was going to marry her mysterious friend James—she just hadn't informed him yet. Also, unlike Bonnie, she had a fatal flaw in her small body.

In *Secret Vampire*, I knew I was dealing with a serious issue: terminal cancer in a high school girl. So I did a lot of research before deciding on a type of cancer that would be truly inoperable and give Poppy only a month or two to live. I went to several hospitals to talk to nurses in oncology wards. I always brought toys for the hospitalized children, but the whole subject was so heartbreaking I was almost afraid to tackle it. Once I did, though, I found that Poppy was even stronger than I had imagined. In the book, she makes the only choice she can to go on living, and she never looks back.

Poppy is one of my favorite girls, and she ushers in Ash Redfern, who quickly became one of my favorite bad boys. Ash has a murky past of womanizing and . . . well, more womanizing. Ash returns in *Daughters of Darkness* because he has been ordered by the leader of all vampires, Hunter Redfern, to bring his three runaway sisters back to their cloistered vampire island. But when Ash locates his sisters, he runs straight into the human stargazer Mary-Lynnette, and the sparks begin flying—literally.

Mary-Lynnette is a character I made up when I was a kid, and I'm always surprised by how many people like her and Ash together. Mary-Lynnette spends most of the time expressing her feelings for Ash by kicking him in the shins, but their dialogues are some of my favorite passages in the whole series.

Ash, in turn, escorts Quinn into the series. And Quinn (who does have a first name, though he rarely uses it) is one really scary guy. A vampire since 1639 A.D., Quinn is sharp, cold, humorless, and heartless.

Unlike Ash, who is mainly guilty of an incredibly long series of one-night stands, Quinn enters the series as a human slave trader. That is, he provides vampires with young girls, and he doesn't ask questions about what happens to the girls afterward. This led to a problem: How on earth was I going to redeem this villain enough to make him someone's soulmate in *The Chosen*?

I really sweated over that. My first task was to make Quinn more sympathetic. The best way to do it seemed to be by telling a bit of Quinn's own tragic story: how he falls in love with sweet Dove Redfern, and how her vampire father decides to make Quinn his heir.

Dove's father is Hunter Redfern, one of the most important vampire leaders in Night World history. This is the same Hunter Redfern who, nearly half a millennium later, sends Ash to drag his sisters back home. The same Hunter Redfern who sends his daughter, Lily, after Jez in *Huntress*. The same Hunter Redfern who tries to turn Delos into a merciless killer in *Black Dawn*.

But, as a boy, Quinn doesn't know anything about the Night World, and he is deeply in love with gentle Dove. When Hunter makes him a vampire by force and then when Quinn can't save Dove from being killed, Quinn's heart freezes over. For four hundred years it accumulates ice—until he meets Rashel.

That's another favorite scene of mine: when Rashel, a dedicated vampire hunter since (guess who?) Hunter Redfern killed her mother, encounters Quinn. A group of Rashel's fellow vampire slayers have captured Quinn and plan to torture him, and Rashel is left alone to guard him. Quinn, feeling old and tired despite his youthful appearance and great power, gives himself up for dead—and is a little glad to do so. Rashel, however, can't stomach the idea of torture. When Rashel talks to this most-hated vampire and hears his story, she deliberately sets him free. And that astonishes him. But it's the soulmate principle working its magic. I loved making two such strong-willed enemies succumb to the silver cord that connects them. I especially loved hearing Quinn warning Rashel not to let him go—and then protecting her when her comrades arrive back in time to see that she's let him loose.

I *really* loved writing about Quinn and Rashel's soulmate sequences.

As Rashel enters Quinn's mind, she sees "thorny scary parts" but also "rainbow places that were aching to grow" and "other parts that seemed to quiver with light, desperate to be awakened." She begins to think that people ask so little of themselves. If the mind of a slave trader can look like this, an ordinary person must have the power to become a saint. It is with this revelation (and much penance on Quinn's part) that Quinn is redeemed.

That's the thread that binds all the novels together: redemption. The possibility of a second chance. Everyone has choices to make, but even the most evil of vampires can choose to atone and be redeemed. It may not necessarily stave off punishment in this world or the next, but redemption *is* possible.

I've been asked who my favorite characters are, and the answer always changes because it depends on the book I'm writing. Right now my favorites are three characters from *Strange Fate*.

As for my favorite couples in the published books? Morgead and Jez—I suppose. Who would find themselves at greater odds than a vampire gang leader and his onetime superior, a vampire who finds out she is half human? I learned some cool martial arts moves as a bonus for writing about them.

Then there is Keller, one of my all-time favorite heroines, and Iliana, the beautiful Witch Child, and Galen, ruler of the shapeshifters: the love triangle in *Witchlight*. Keller starts out seeming brusque and businesslike, but the love of Galen and of the unselfish Iliana help to heal her inner wounds.

And I can't forget Thierry and Hannah, and Circle Daybreak. I created Circle Daybreak because the Night World witches had only two clans: Circle Twilight and Circle Midnight. Those, like Thea in *Spellbinder*, who belong to Circle Twilight are not-so-wicked witches (that is, they don't want to exterminate all humans like the darkest witches, those who belong to Circle Midnight), but they are still wicked enough.

So what was to be done with all these new soulmates, when Night World law said that they must be put to death? Someone had to make a place for them where they would be safe, and I decided it was Thierry, one of the oldest vampires, and Hannah, his Old Soul soulmate, who has lived hundreds of lifetimes without ever reaching the age of seventeen. They are the ones who revive Circle Daybreak, where humans and Night People can forget about past tragedies and concentrate on a brighter future together.

Although Thierry is an old vampire, he isn't the *oldest* vampire. There is one older, the one who Changed him. She provides another thread that binds the series: the pitiless Maya. Maya is the first vampire, the witch who finds the secret of eternal life—and chooses to use it for evil. But there will be plenty more about her, including a look at the *young* Maya, her sister Hellewise, and their mother, Hecate Witch-Queen, in the upcoming *Strange Fate*.

And so now I've come full circle, back to *Strange Fate*. But I can't finish until I add the other joy that the re-release of Night World has brought me. It's brought me into contact with *you* by e-mail. Night World fans write so many intelligent, articulate, courteous, exciting e-mails! I love to get messages from "old" fans, who say my works "got them through high school." Thank you for them! And messages from new fans, who say they have just read all my reissued books—and are impatient for more. Thank you! And the messages that simply demand: "When is *Strange Fate* coming out?" Thank you, too!

With a full heart, all I can say is thank you, thank you, and thank you again! I never thought I would have a chance to write an open letter to all Night World fans, and I can only wish that you knew how grateful I am . . . for this second chance.

Sincerely,

Lisa J Smith

P.S. I love to get e-mail, letters, and messages. Visit me at ljanesmith.net!

Vampires

How can one recognize a vampire? Not easily. Although *all* Night People are extremely beautiful, they work very hard to avoid detection. Vampires appear mostly human and ordinary, albeit mysterious. But in preparation for their daily feeding, vampires' incisors grow long and curved, and their irises can turn silver. Their presence takes on a savage air. And they become visibly cunning.

Vampires are predators with incredibly fast reflexes, enabling them to strike their prey with great speed and accuracy. But vampires do not need to kill to satiate their hunger. A vampire can feed on a mortal creature's blood without completely draining its life. Depending on the size of the beast, a vampire may need to feed on a few animals to get his or her daily sustenance. Some vampires prefer human blood; others enjoy animal blood. It's all a matter of taste. Just as a vampire's wounds heal quickly, so too do the puncture wounds from a vampire bite.

Vampires can communicate telepathically among themselves and can also use these powers for mind control. Mind control rarely, if ever, works on fellow Night People but is quite effective on humans. Vampires primarily exert this power when they want a stubborn human to comply with their wishes. Humans register a vampire's telepathic communication as their own internal thought.

Some vampires go so far as to purge an incident from a human's memory. Humans experience this as "lost time." Most notably, Rowan, Kestrel, and Jade erase Vic's and Todd's memory of picking up these three hitchhiking sisters in *Daughters of Darkness*, and Jez cleans the human gang leader's memory in *Huntress*. Jez touches the human's forehead to erase the memory of their encounter, actually changing the chemistry of his thoughts in the process.

Vampires are a primal clan and are not to be provoked. They are often willful and would rather fight to the death than admit they are wrong. Most vampires enjoy a good hunt and make formidable opponents as they employ their acute senses to track scents and movements. Their eyesight is particularly impressive, and although vampires are sensitive to the daylight, they have no physical need to be nocturnal. All vampires are vulnerable to wood and fire. But within this clan of immortal Night People, there are two distinct kinds of vampires: those who are born vampires, called lamia, and those who are Changed, called made vampires.

Lamia

Lamia assemble at the sign of the black iris and believe themselves to be the superior vampires. Power and entitlement are passed from generation to generation through this patriarchal community, and lamia view their heritage as a right to dominance.

When lamia choose to reproduce, their offspring are also vampires. These family vampires, as they are called, can grow old but have the ability to physically stop aging whenever they chose. Some vampires who are hundreds of years old appear to be toddlers or teenagers, but a vampire who decides to stop aging must be cautious. Should he or she choose to resume aging, the process speeds forward exponentially, which, as Kestrel remarks, "if you've been alive for five or six hundred years can be quite interesting."

Night World vampires are traditionally named for natural elements such as gems, flowers, and trees. Although wood is deadly for both types of vampires, lamia named after a tree are said to have increased powers.

Lamia dominate the Elder Council, an elite group governing all vampires. Hunter Redfern leads the Council, if not by title, by the sheer force of his personality. This Council sets decrees on subjects such as feeding and marriage. One law prohibits mercy killings for humans, as Dr. Rasmussen tells his son James, who discovers his best friend is terminally ill. The Elder Council also holds trials for those who break Night World and clan laws. When Hodge Burdock stands trial for telling a human about the Night World, he is burned alive at the Elder Council's order.

The members of the Elder Council also participate in the Night World Council, or Joint Council. The Joint Council has representatives from each clan and passes laws by which all Night People must abide. The Night World Council is credited for ending the human slave trade run by vampires in medieval times—not out of sympathy for humans, but rather to protect the Night World from the increased danger of exposure from the practice.

NOTABLE LAMIA

Red Fern: Maya's son, the first born vampire, and the namesake of this most illustrious vampire family, Red holds a special place in lamia lore. Red receives his name because of the flaming color of his hair, a trait that is passed down through the millennium in the Redfern line.

Hunter Redfern: Descendent of Red Fern, Hunter creates an enclave of vampires near Maine during colonial times. Crediting his daughter Dove's staking as the impetus, Hunter presides over the island, which still operates like it is the sixteenth century and has very strict rules about dress, entertainment, and marriage. Hunter is a vicious vampire, willing to forge a bloodfeast alliance with made vampires to ensure that the conservative traditions of Night World are preserved.

Ash Redfern: Handsome like James Dean, this vampire is wickedly charming and—well, just plain wicked. Ash acts as the head of the Redfern family on the West Coast and is quick to defend Night

World laws, but the Elders believe he is "*too* liberal" in his associations with people on the Outside and in befriending werewolves. And that's *before* Ash discovers his soulmate is human!

Morgead Blackthorn: Not all lamia are Redferns, but Morgead demonstrates that all vampires (at least male vampires) share a proclivity toward competition and arrogance. Morgead's protectiveness of Jez, however, does not stem from arrogance. His is the love of a soulmate.

NIGHT WORLD ETIQUETTE

You are going to visit a fellow friend from the Night World. When you arrive at her house, you

A. ring the front doorbell. It is rude to enter unannounced.

B. ring the front doorbell, but don't wait for acknowledgment before entering.

C. let yourself in the back door. After all, you're friends, right?

D. telepathically let your friend know you've arrived, so she is standing at the door to greet you.

E. use the door, front or back, that is marked with a black flower.

ANSWER: E

Everyone knows vampires can come and go as they please in the Night World and don't need an invitation to enter a house! And while it is polite to ring the bell and wait for your friend to answer (even Blaise wouldn't expect a friend to be waiting at the door—unless maybe it was raining), a true Night Person always knocks and enters through the door marked with a black flower.

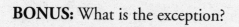

BONUS: What is the exception?

ANSWER: It is possible to bury an enchanted amulet on someone's property for protection. Then all Night Creatures must be invited inside before they can cross the threshold. Thierry buries an amulet like this in Hannah Snow's yard to try to protect her from Maya in *Soulmate*.

Poppy's twin brother Phillip is a go-getter. As a junior at El Camino High, he stars on three sports teams, serves as the class president, and earns a 4.0 for the year. Just *thinking* about all of that could make you tired. His secret? Phil knows how to start the morning right. He always reads the newspaper while eating the most important meal of the day. **What's Phil's breakfast of champions?**

ANSWER: Special K

BONUS: So who eats Wheaties for breakfast
in *Secret Vampire*?

ANSWER: James

BONUS: What does Poppy eat for breakfast right before she discovers she is sick?

ANSWER: A single Frosted Flake

What is the one party that Iliana *doesn't* want to attend?

A. Jaime and Brett Ashton Hughes's birthday party
B. The Solstice Ceremony
C. The prom
D. A holiday party
E. Homecoming

ANSWER: B

Iliana is slow to embrace her role as a Wild Power and the Witch Child and has no interest in attending the Solstice Ceremony. After all, it is the same night as Jaime and Brett's party! And she *really* doesn't want to participate in the Promise Ceremony, which would betroth her to Galen, unifying the witches and the shapeshifters.

Who is "every bloodsucking leech's worst enemy"?

A. Ash
B. Jez
C. Rashel
D. Keller
E. Galen

ANSWER: C

Rashel is a vampire hunter on a mission for revenge! After a vampire viciously kills her mother and her Aunt Connie, Rashel knows she has to be strong, channel her anger, and learn to defend herself. Rashel stakes her first vampire when she is twelve and swiftly builds a reputation as a fierce vampire slayer.

In *Huntress*, signs that the Old Powers are rising include

- A. disease.
- B. natural disasters.
- C. animal attacks.
- D. the soulmate principle.
- E. all of the above.

ANSWER: E

The Old Powers aren't people but natural forces: ancient magic. Dormant since humans began to populate the earth in large numbers, the Old Powers start to show signs of reappearing. Disease, natural disasters, animal attacks—even the rise of the soulmate principle—are indicators that a revolution is coming. . . .

KNOW YOUR LINGO

"We promise to be kin to you . . ." To continue the blood-tie ceremony one says the following:

- A. "to protect and defend you always."
- B. "now and forever more."
- C. "for Hecate proclaimed it."
- D. "until the apocalypse arrives."
- E. "by the power vested in us by Hellewise."

ANSWER: A

The kinship ceremony is an ancient ceremony in Night World tradition that joins two families through the exchange of blood. Unlike the exchanges needed to "make" a vampire, this ritual only necessitates a few drops, as it is mostly symbolic. Rowan, Kestrel, and Jade create an alliance with Mary-Lynnette and Mark in *Daughters of Darkness*. Together, they say these words: "We promise to be kin to you, to protect and defend you always."

"Even if you kill her. She will still be alive—here."

These impassioned words from Thierry in *Soulmate* are so heartfelt they bring tears to Hannah's eyes. Trapped in the abandoned silver mine, Thierry tries to protect Hannah from the vengeful Maya. But Maya is determined that *this* time Hannah will die . . . and stay dead. So Maya devises a plan to make Hannah into a vampire and then stake her. While Old Souls are humans who reincarnate, vampires don't have the ability to be reborn. As even Maya says, "It's an interesting bit of trivia, isn't it? Maybe it'll be on *Jeopardy!* someday."

Made Vampires

Once living creatures needing to breathe oxygen and eat food to stay alive, made vampires are Changed into the undead by other vampires. Humans can be turned into vampires, as can other Night People, and any vampire, lamia or made, can initiate this conversion.

Transforming into a vampire is a grueling process, and one must be young and fit to endure the physical strain. Teens are resilient enough to undergo the Change, but even they encounter serious risks. As vampires are made by the exchange of blood, a vampire must drink a human's blood—and a human must drink a vampire's blood. If too much blood is taken at one time from either party, the side effects can range from light-headedness to death. Humans find vampire blood to be incredibly energizing, and their senses are dramatically heightened to be like a vampire's after the exchange.

Nibbled humans, like Poppy and Mary-Lynnette, say a vampire bite initially feels like a bee or jellyfish sting, but then the pain subsides and warmth radiates at the incision. As one goes through the transformation, that person becomes both physically and emotionally close to the vampire initiating the Change, seeing into the vampire's mind and feeling the impression of the vampire's being during the exchanges. If the human makes the Change willingly, this can be a transcendental experience. If the transformation is made maliciously, it can be pure torture.

Made vampires stop aging after they are Changed. They die as humans and awaken as vampires, their bodies forever preserved at the age of their transformation. Poppy will always appear just shy of seventeen years old; Timmy will always look a mere four years old.

Made vampires recognize one another by the sign of the black rose they wear on their clothing or jewelry, and they are an interesting group. There are many remarkable and influential made vampires, but a majority of these vampires were not raised in the Night World tradition. Those with the approval of the Elders have earned their way into the Night World, despite their human origins. Others try to stay on the outskirts of Night World, as unsanctioned vampires will surely receive a death sentence if detected by the Elders.

NOTABLE MADE VAMPIRES

Maya, daughter of Hecate Witch-Queen: Maya's first wish is to be immortal, and with elaborate spells, Maya attains her dream—at a price. She must drink blood daily. Maya is the *first* made vampire. Her son Red Fern is the first born vampire. Maya is ruthless and vindictive and excruciatingly beautiful with dark hair and a willowy figure. She also craves attention.

Thierry Descouedres: The second made vampire, Thierry is Changed by a jealous Maya, who is determined that Thierry love her more than her sister. But after Maya transforms Thierry, he feels no compassion toward her. Instead, he is struck with hatred. Theirs becomes a battle of the ages as Thierry, Lord of the Night World, tries to unite with his soulmate, and Maya uses all of her powers to keep the two apart, millennium after millennium.

Poppy North: The Elders would never have approved of Poppy's transformation. Opposed to humans becoming part of the Night World, the Elders would not condone James's actions—even if he is rescuing his soulmate. Poppy and James's relationship is one of the first indicators that the soulmate principle is on the rise—and Poppy is perhaps the most famous modern made vampire in Circle Daybreak.

John Quinn: Quinn is not pleased about making the Change. He's been eighteen for four centuries and he is *still* bitter. Quinn is turned into a vampire by Hunter Redfern, who believes that he has no living sons and is desperate for Quinn to become his heir. Although Quinn does not bear the Redfern last name, he is considered to be a full-blooded Redfern and sits on the Elder Council.

YOU MIGHT BE A VAMPIRE IF . . .

* you don't wear sunglasses *just* to look cool.
* you are a wiz at Ping-Pong.
* you've contemplated a career in psychology
  or interior design.
* you are very stubborn—and very good at convincing
  people to see things your way.
* you don't get cold, regardless of the weather.
* you are not tempted by sweets.

Why does Mrs. Burdock keep goats in *Daughters of Darkness*?

ANSWER: If you ask Claudine, Mary-Lynnette's stepmother, why her neighbor keeps goats, she will probably tell you it is for the milk they produce. Maybe even the company they provide.

Although milk may have a lot of calcium and protein for humans, Opal Burdock keeps goats for an entirely different kind of nutrition. Mrs. Burdock needs the hemoglobin in the goats' blood to stay healthy. As a vampire living outside the Night World domain, Mrs. B's goats provide a steady source of nutrition that won't cause a stir in the community. She can discreetly feed on them without arousing suspicion from the other residents of Briar Creek—very important when you are the only vampire living in a small town! Plus Mrs. B is aging, so she needs to access a source of blood near her house because she can't go into the woods to hunt.

BONUS: Jade, a vampire and Mrs. Burdock's niece, keeps a cat. Is Tiggy pet or prey?

ANSWER: Jade fawns over her little black kitten.
Tiggy is definitely a pet.

When does Poppy first fall in love with James?

    A. When Poppy learns he can save her from a painful death.

    B. When James uses mind control to convince Poppy they are a match.

    C. When James gets nervous and spills his lunch in Poppy's lap.

    D. Poppy falls for James when she is five.

    E. Poppy has a crush on James, but she knows it is true love when they kiss.

ANSWER: D

When James explains the soulmate principle to Poppy, she claims, "I *always* knew you were perfect for me." She says she's known since she was five, when she first met James.

In kindergarten James was a little strange, and he always got picked on by the playground bullies. Poppy wouldn't stand for it—"even at five she'd had a great right hook." Poppy defended James and afterward asked him, "Wanna be friends?" From then on the two were inseparable.

Grandma Harman is killed by

A. a hit-and-run driver.
B. Blue Fire.
C. a silver picture frame.
D. a train.
E. two werewolves and a tiger.

ANSWER: E

Three shapeshifters ambush Grandma (Edgith) Harman, the oldest witch in the world, on the sidewalk outside her shop. Gran Harman dies, and the entire witch clan goes into mourning for their Crone. Circle Daybreakers, however, fear additional threats. If these 'shifters are willing to attack in the open, then the powers are shifting—and new alliances need to be forged.

Rashel believes *zanshin* is integral to being a good vampire hunter. What is it?

A. A special kind of wooden handcuff
B. A state of total awareness
C. A Japanese sword
D. A ring that protects whoever wears it
E. A breastplate of silver worn underneath one's clothing

ANSWER: B

Although Rashel's favorite weapon for fighting vampires is a wooden *booken*, a long, curved Japanese sword with a sharp edge, she also uses *zanshin* in combat. Rashel knows that *zanshin*, a state of total awareness, is imperative for outsmarting and outmaneuvering creatures in the Night World. From Japanese martial arts, *zanshin* requires that one be fully present in an action from start to finish—and that one be aware of others' actions, in case they should attack.

"Do it quickly . . ."

In *Huntress*, Jez Redfern corners a gang leader in Muir Woods who whimpers this sentence. Instantly, Jez is flashed back to her childhood when her mother uttered the same words while reasoning with an attacker to spare her daughter's life.

Jez always believed vampire hunters had slain her parents. But as this particular memory unfolds, Jez realizes it was vampires who made her an orphan—vampires who fault Jez for being part-vampire and part-human. With this revelation, Jez, who has long been a huntress, must face her mixed-race heritage and re-evaluate her future. All because of these three words.

Ghouls

Ghouls are a particularly nasty sect of the undead. These gruesome creatures didn't quite complete the transformation into vampires and are caught between immortal life and imminent decay. Most ghouls were once innocent humans who became victims of overfeeding vampires or of careless vampires who didn't heed the known age restrictions for transformation.

Ghouls have an insatiable thirst for blood, which consumes all of their focus, making them rather clueless. They smell of rot and, like a vampire, must be killed with a wooden stake through the heart.

YOU MIGHT BE A GHOUL IF . . .

* you love *Night of the Living Dead* and reruns of the *Twilight Zone*!
* you don't bother with perfume because you have a very distinctive scent.
* you constantly feel like your body is going to fall apart. (Could you be getting the flu?)
* you aren't depressed but just don't feel alive in the way you used to.
* you feel a strange closeness with compost.
* you are perpetually thirsty, for blood, that is.

Why does Gran Harman live in Las Vegas?

ANSWER: Las Vegas, with its large transient population, is a Night World hot spot! Many vampires move there to feed on humans—humans who won't be missed if they disappear. Witches are also drawn to Vegas, but for the power vortexes located in the desert surrounding the city.

But Gran Harman? She lives in Vegas for the weather. Having developed breathing problems as a child, this Crone loves the dry air and warm temperatures that help to improve her health.

BONUS: Where is the most exotic place in Vegas?

ANSWER: According to Thea, the most exotic place in Las Vegas is a modest house with real trees in the yard: a human's house. Eric's house, to be precise.

Who creates the Dark Kingdom and builds Black Dawn?

A. Hunter Redfern
B. Lily Redfern
C. Chervil Redfern
D. Jez Redfern
E. Delos Redfern

ANSWER: C

Chervil Redfern and his father, Hunter, share a short temper and ill will. When the two become estranged, Chervil abandons his family to start his own monarchy of Night People with his friends. In the Dark Kingdom, Chervil raises Delos, his son, using intimidation and punishment, and without Hunter's knowledge. Chervil commands Delos to use his Blue Fire to his own ends, much to the young Prince Delos's emotional and physical detriment.

Blaise and Thea are two of the last Harman girls directly descended from Hellewise. What lost witch can trace her matrilineal lineage back to Hellewise?

A. Tanya Jun
B. Gillian Lennox
C. Amy Nowick
D. Sylvia Weald
E. Mary-Lynnette Carter

ANSWER: B

Gillian Lennox learns about her witch lineage after completing her first spells. Using two wax figurines to represent her rivals, Gillian enacts spells that give Tanya a rash and cause Kimberly to lose her voice. Angel praises Gillian for her good work, then reveals that Gillian is a "full-fledged witch." Gillian's great-grandmother Elspeth was a Hearth-Woman, descended from the revered mother of all witches, Hellewise.

Mary-Lynnette likes to solve mysteries.
Who is her favorite detective?

A. Sherlock Holmes
B. Nancy Drew
C. Perry Mason
D. Miss Marple
E. Encyclopedia Brown

ANSWER: B

Mary-Lynnette is quite the sleuth! She frequently references Nancy Drew, wondering what the girl detective would do if she were in Mary-Lynnette's situation. Inspired by Nancy, Mary-Lynnette decides to investigate when she sees three girls burying a big black plastic bag in Mrs. Burdock's backyard. And when Mary-Lynnette and the Redferns speak with Jeremy at the gas station, she faults herself for not thinking up a cover story ahead of time because "Nancy Drew would definitely have thought of that."

"Go mark a fire hydrant or something."

It doesn't take a vampire's heightened sensitivity to sniff out the werewolf in this quote. But to which werewolf is this remark addressed?

He was in human form at the time he spoke these words, but you may remember Ulf as the first werewolf to appear in the Night World series. Despite his lanky appearance, Ulf works as a bouncer at the Black Iris.

And who says it? James in *Secret Vampire*.

Witches

Witches have an innate ability to draw on their inner strength to effect magic through spells and chants. Enchantments are often produced with simple words and intense focus, but many are accompanied by fire, a complicated assortment of ingredients, and a physical representation of those to be changed by the charm. Members of this clan can call upon Hecate, the first and most powerful witch, for power. They can also call upon their *own power* as daughters and sons of Hecate when casting spells, as demonstrated by Thea in *Spellbinder*.

Some witches also have prophetic visions—either brief glimpses into the future or puzzling revelations that must be unraveled with careful study. Witches who have these tendencies are usually unable to guide or extend their visions, but as this power is rare, prophetic witches are revered and hold a distinctive place in the hierarchy.

This clan is a matrilineal society that celebrates women, and the most powerful witches are the Crone, the Mother, and the Maiden. The witches with these titles have demonstrated their awesome powers for enacting spells and witnessing visions. Witches age like humans with regard to physical appearance and life span, so the Maiden is expected to one day become the Mother, then the Crone. The Crone is the leader of the Inner Circle, a group akin to the Vampire's Elder Council.

The Inner Circle is a governing body composed of nine of the most powerful witches in Night World. As Thea describes with awe, "These people were the witch geniuses, the prodigies and the sages, the far-seers, the teachers, the policy-makers." Despite the matriarchal emphasis of this clan, the Circle consists of both women and men. In addition to Grandma Harman, the Crone; Mother Cybele, the Mother; and Aradia, the Maiden, the other members of the Circle are Rhys, Belfana, Creon, Old Bob, Ursula, and Nana Buruku.

The rest of the witches in the Night World divide themselves between those who practice moderate magic, Circle Twilight, and those who practice the darkest magic, Circle Midnight. All of the Circles mark themselves with the sign of the black dahlia and are sensitive to iron. And all witches can communicate telepathically among themselves.

Psychics are a subgroup of witches whose powers lie dormant, waiting to be discovered. Psychics have been raised outside of the Night World and are ignorant of their legacy. Some psychics, like Poppy North and Gillian Lennox, find their way into the Night World fold by accident. Others, like Gary Fargeon and Iliana Harman, are sought out by their clan—traced through family and welcomed to their birthright. But some, having only moderate powers or suppressing their talents for fear of being ostracized by their human peers, never connect with the Night World.

NOTABLE WITCHES

Hellewise Hearth-Woman: Hellewise, the daughter of Hecate Witch-Queen, lives during the Stone Age and is worshiped as the head of the Harman family, the most powerful family of witches. Hellewise is frequently called upon as a source of power in casting and is admired for her benevolence and beauty.

Maeve Harman: The mother of Hunter Redfern's daughters, Lily, Garnet, Dove, and Roseclear, Maeve casts the protective spell on the haven that Hunter creates for vampires. Her spell staves off human interference, protecting the Night World residents from discovery. Maeve is not fond of Hunter, despite their blood-tie, and raises their youngest daughter as a witch far from the enclave.

Blaise and Thea Harman: The granddaughters of the Crone, Blaise and Thea are cousins and the end of the Harman line. With personalities as opposite as night and day, these two gals are at once intense rivals and best friends.

Phillip North: The brother of the well-known made vampire Poppy North, Phil is a psychic who discovers his witch heritage. Linked to the Night World through his father's family, Phil is glad to learn why he can telepathically communicate with his sister—but has no interest in exploring his witch powers.

YOU MIGHT BE A WITCH IF . . .

* you have a knack for knowing something is going to happen before it actually does.
* your spice rack is overflowing with different herbs.
* you can telepathically communicate with animals.
* your favorite shape is a circle.
* you have an enchanting personality.
* you are *always* in touch with your inner goddess.

Who is Paula Belizer and what happens to her in *Dark Angel*?

ANSWER: Paula Belizer is the young girl who disappears from Gillian Lennox's small town in southwestern Pennsylvania. Paula is killed by a spell cast by renegade witch Gary Fargeon.

Gary experiments with a fire elemental, a very dangerous spell that burns white with heat, when he is alone in the woods. But Paula runs through the woods after her dog, accidentally breaking the circle. Gary loses control of the flame, and Paula is killed on contact.

Not knowing what to do, Gary buries Paula in the snow. Gary dies later that night in a car crash. A year later, with some persuasion, Gary tells Gillian where Paula's body is located, so Paula's parents can have closure and Gary's spirit can find peace.

Rowan, Kestrel, and Jade's father thinks his daughters are disobedient because

    A. they refuse to go to school.

    B. of the stars' unusual alignment when each was born.

    C. of an ancient blood-tie ceremony linking vampires and witches.

    D. the girls feed only on large game.

    E. Kestrel, who was adopted from a werewolf family, is a bad influence.

ANSWER: C

Rowan, Kestral, and Jade's father blames their disobedience on a kinship ceremony performed in the sixteenth century. At that time, the Redfern line was in danger because Hunter Redfern's son had disappeared and Hunter couldn't produce a new heir. To secure this vampire's ancient legacy, Hunter performed a blood-tie ceremony with a witch. Descendants on both sides share a hint of blood from the other clan. (In *Spellbinder*, you'll remember Thea and Blaise mentioning they have a bit of vampire in them.) Vampires look down on witches and their matrilineal society, so the girls' father blames their wild behavior on this blood tie.

What is Poppy's first thought after her first kiss?

    A. "And I'm comatose. Great."
    B. "I wish it would last forever."
    C. "James's mouth tastes sweet—for a vampire."
    D. "I'm floating. This must be true love."
    E. "Now we can never just be friends. . . ."

ANSWER: A

James first kisses Poppy after they complete the last exchange of blood that will turn Poppy into a vampire. James cradles Poppy as soft music plays from her CD *Music to Disappear In*. Poppy struggles to open her eyes to tell a concerned James, "I'm all right. Just . . . sleepy." That is when James settles Poppy on her pillows and kisses her on the forehead, and Poppy thinks, "And I'm comatose. Great."

As a member of the First House of Shapeshifters, Galen has the power to choose his transformational animal. He decides to change into

A. an eagle.
B. a lion.
C. a giraffe.
D. a dove.
E. a leopard.

ANSWER: E

Galen originally wants to take the shape of a peaceful creature, yet in the heat of battle he takes Keller's impression and shifts into a leopard. Galen's leopard, with beautiful golden tones, shares the same coloring as his person. As a leopard Galen is able to defend Keller, his soulmate, and Iliana, the mysterious Witch Child, in battle against the dragon in *Witchlight*.

"This kitten has claws."

After killing a vampire, Rashel's ritual is to mark the newly mummified body with a back scratcher. Then she says, "This kitten has claws."

Why is this part of Rashel's mantra? Rashel's mother nicknamed her Kitten, and the ritual is a way to honor the memory of her mother. Rashel is known by the Night World community as The Cat for this practice and Rashel likes the ironic nod to Catwoman.

Shapeshifters

Shapeshifters play a complicated role in Night World society. They are at once the most powerful and the most despised clan. The dragons' brute force made shapeshifters dominant, but throughout the ages, the malicious abuse of power by *all* shapeshifters made them "the lowest of all the Night People."

Shapeshifters have four main divisions in their race: those who can choose the animal they shift into, those whose shape was determined for them, werewolves (see page 95), and dragons (see page 113). Because of these four subdivisions, shapeshifters do not always act as a unified group.

Members of the First House of Shapeshifters, the Drache family, have the ability to determine their shape. It is a decision that must be made carefully—as it cannot be reversed. To transform for the first time, a shapeshifter of this heritage must touch the animal he or she wants to shift into. Most of the Draches turn into warring beasts, and they have a reputation for exerting their power unilaterally. These 'shifters don't show allegiance to the Night World or Circle Daybreak. Their loyalty falls with whomever they believe will win the battle at hand. Slow to make pacts with others, these shapeshifters are firmly committed to the cause when they do.

Those whose shape is determined for them—at birth or by the bite of a 'shifter who is in animal form—become animals with great presence, such as jungle cats or bears or birds of prey.

The ability to shift between human and animal forms is innate, but not without complications. Shapeshifters can get stuck between shapes. 'Shifters are taught never to transform in front of people, rather to change in safe, discreet places. A great deal of energy is released when one shapeshifts. According to Keller, a 'shifting panther, changing is "painful in a nice way, like the feeling of having a tight bandage removed. A release."

As shapeshifters spend much of their time in human form, they frequently wear clothing that is made from the hair and hides of other shapeshifters. This enables them to change smoothly and efficiently, without ripping or ruining their "people clothing." A seamless transformation is important if a shapeshifter is trying to protect someone or defend something.

NOTABLE SHAPESHIFTERS

Rasha Keller: Stuck in mid-shift with cat ears and a tail, Keller is abandoned by her human parent as a baby. After being rescued and raised by Circle Daybreak, Keller decides to work for the organization to pay them back for taking care of her as a child. Like the cat she shifts into, Keller is always very independent.

Galen Drache: The descendant of dragons and other demonic creatures, Galen tries to reject his powers in favor of a more positive life. He wants to choose an animal that demonstrates peace, not enacts violence, when deciding his shifting shape. But he can't escape his role in the First House of the Shapeshifters. Promised to the Witch Child, Galen is called to unify the witches and the 'shifters in *Witchlight*.

NIGHT WORLD ETIQUETTE

How do you greet a witch?

A. "Descendant of Hecate, salutations."
B. "Hocus-pocus."
C. "Unity."
D. "Kinship."
E. The same way you would any other
Night Person or human.

ANSWER: C

"Unity" is the proper way to greet a fellow witch. It is an ancient address that demonstrates the promise of oneness and harmony among this Night World clan. When witches part company, they say, "Merry meet and merry part and merry meet again."

How does Quinn get the scar in his side?

ANSWER: When Quinn awakes in the Redfern household after being made into a vampire, he is livid. And afraid. Quinn's father, a Puritan minister, is the only person Quinn thinks might be able to help him now that he is "a monster. An unholy creature who needed blood to survive." Dove Redfern, a born vampire and Quinn's true love, pleads with him not to go, but to no avail. Instead Dove agrees to accompany Quinn to his home in the hope that he will be calmed.

Quinn is right. His father knows what to do. He grabs a wooden stake from the fire, determined to purge the devil from their bodies. Quinn's father impales Dove, and Quinn gets the scar in his side as he tries to shield her from the blow. Dove dies, Quinn escapes, and thereafter he vows to sever ties with the human race.

While Jez sometimes has difficulty sharing her feelings, she admits to loving

    A. Hugh Davis.
    B. her Harley 883 Sportster Hugger.
    C. Morgead Blackthorn.
    D. all of the above.
    E. none of the above.

ANSWER: D

Jez loves Hugh Davis for befriending her when she arrives at her Uncle Jim's family home. She doesn't know any humans at the time, and other members of Circle Daybreak don't yet trust her. Jez also loves her Harley, describing it as "her steel and chrome thoroughbred." Last, but certainly not least, Jez loves Morgead. Of the three, Jez is *in love with* Morgead, her soulmate. She just doesn't realize it until Morgead is in danger.

Maya is a formidable character in the Night World. She is

A. a witch.
B. a vampire.
C. a werewolf.
D. a shapeshifter.
E. all of the above.

ANSWER: E

Maya is a fierce power, arguably the most ferocious creature of the Night. Maya begins her life as a witch, just like her sister Hellewise. But an intense desire to be immortal drives Maya to cast a spell that turns her into the first vampire. Maya now can live forever, provided she drinks human blood each day. Among the powers Maya has are those of a shapeshifter and a werewolf. Maya uses these powers of transformation while hunting Hana of Three Rivers and Hannah Snow's other incarnations.

Who is the "princess of forbidden spells"?

A. Aradia
B. Aunt Ursula
C. Blaise
D. Iliana
E. Thea

ANSWER: E

Thea and Eric break one of Night World's cardinal laws when they fall in love. And when Thea and Blaise brainstorm ways to protect Eric from the Night World, Thea refers to herself as the "princess of forbidden spells." Thea has already cast a powerful and illegal spell to call back a spirit. But she is willing to risk even *more* trouble with the Elders if it means protecting Eric!

"She will come clothed in flowers, shod in blue and scarlet, and she will speak of freedom."

Maggie's blue cotton slouch sock and red velveteen anklet pairing are quite a fashion statement! When Maggie falls asleep in her pajamas doing homework, she never dreams she'll set off on a quest to another world to find her missing brother. But lucky for her, Maggie's mismatched outfit identifies her as the Deliverer in the Dark Kingdom, gaining her recognition and much-needed help on her journey. A slave named only the Soaker is the first to recognize Maggie from the prophecy, and she rejoices that Maggie has arrived to save the slaves at Black Dawn and pledges to help Maggie however she can.

KNOW YOUR LINGO

How does the Crone greet people?

A. "Good tidings, friends."

B. "Unity, I speak with the voice of Hecate."

C. "I, Crone of the house of Harman, am pleased to meet you."

D. "The Goddess's bright blessing on you all."

E. "May you find comfort in the daylight, serenity in the night."

ANSWER: D

In *Witchlight*, Grandma Harman makes the trip from Nevada to North Carolina to meet Iliana. The matriarch of the witches, Grandma Harman is very old and very influential. She uses the greeting "The Goddess's bright blessing on you all," demonstrating her allegiance to the otherworldly powers and her benevolence.

Werewolves

Humans that change into wolves at the full moon? Not in the Night World! No, the members of this clan are werewolves through and through. They are feral canines that shapeshift to look like humans, and they can change regardless of the phase of the moon.

These growling, drooling creatures are an intimidating breed. With large incisors and lean, muscular bodies, they can jump and run and strike with great viciousness. Werewolves hunt to eat, so there is no disguising a werewolf attack. Werewolves feast on an animal's internal organs and have a particular taste for hearts and livers.

Because of their fierce territorial instincts, Night World werewolves are frequently employed in the security industry as bouncers, bodyguards, and henchmen. 'Wolves have a talent for watching and stalking their prey, whether it is an animal in the woods or a human in town. So it is fitting that this clan's symbol is the highly toxic, black foxglove. The flower got its name from an old myth in which foxes magically donned the blooms on their paws so they could creep into henhouses at night and eat the plump birds.

Often considered the lowest class of shapeshifter, this subgroup has not been favored by Night World politics. Werewolves are demeaned partially because they represent a smaller organization of the shape-shifters and partially because their loyalties lie in their individual advancement. Despite there being some upstanding werewolves, most have earned their reputations as sneaky and unstoppable. Unless they see you wielding silver, that is. Silver is fatal to werewolves.

NOTABLE WEREWOLVES

Jeremy Lovett: Mary-Lynnette loves how helpful Jeremy is, carefully washing the windshield of her beat-up station wagon whenever she visits the gas station. But Jeremy never gets too close to anyone. He is a loner—and a renegade werewolf. Jeremy does not adhere to Night World feeding laws, even going so far as to kill his uncle for trying to enforce them. Jeremy also devises some creative ways to intimidate Jade, Kestrel, and Rowan when they move to Briar Creek.

Azarius: This werewolf thug is hired by Lily Redfern to help find the Wild Power in *Huntress*. He has a mangy, dark coat and likes to pick fights. After wrestling with Jez on the BART platform, Azarius happily takes his revenge on the feisty half-breed, helping kidnap Jez and then impaling her. Azarius dies in the Wild Power's Blue Fire.

Lupe Acevedo: Half-werewolf and half-human, Lupe's father is killed by werewolves, but Thierry rescues Lupe and her mother. Lupe becomes a member of Circle Daybreak and goes to work for Thierry, as one of Thierry's bodyguards and as a locator and protector of Hana's reincarnating soul. Lupe is recognizable as a grey-brown 'wolf with amber eyes and strong, graceful legs.

YOU MIGHT BE A WEREWOLF IF . . .

* jewelry stores creep you out.
* you've been mistaken for Sasquatch.
* you have excellent teeth and gums despite never flossing.
* your favorite foods are calves' liver (just barely brushed over a flame, please) and steak tartare.
* when you throw a tantrum, your howling can be heard for miles.

In *Soulmate*, why does Hannah Snow have a birthmark?

ANSWER: Hannah Snow has a birthmark on her left cheek that doctors cannot remove. This rose-colored streak on her pale skin is more than a birthmark: it is a psychic brand. Hannah receives this brand from Thierry during her first lifetime when she is Hana of Three Rivers.

Overtaken by bloodlust, the newly made vampire Thierry attacks everyone in the small village of Three Rivers—including Hana. Thierry comes to his senses moments before Hana dies, but it is too late to save her. Thierry is tortured knowing he has killed an innocent girl, the girl who is his soulmate. As he cradles Hana's dead body, Thierry gently sweeps the hair off her face, leaving a smear of Hana's blood on her cheek. After that, every time Hana of Three Rivers reincarnates, she bears the mark of Thierry's sorrow upon her cheek.

BONUS: How does Hannah feel about her birthmark?

ANSWER: Hannah likes the birthmark. She believes it is the perfect imperfection. It reminds her of who she is and that she is human.

Who does Thea bring back from the dead?

A. Suzanne Blanchet
B. Phoebe Garner
C. Dew Ratih
D. Annie Butter
E. Omiya Inoshishi

ANSWER: A

Thea *intends* to bring back the docile Phoebe Garner, a witch who died of consumption before the Burning Times. But Blaise interrupts Thea's spell. During Blaise's struggle to keep Thea from throwing Phoebe's amulet into the fire, an amulet with a lock of Suzanne Blanchet's hair lands in the flame. And with a great burst of lightning, Suzanne's vengeful spirit is released into the world.

When Maggie first sees Sylvia in the Dark Kingdom, Sylvia is dressed in medieval clothing and has a falcon on her wrist. Who is the shapeshifting falcon?

A. Hunter, Prince Delos's great-grandfather
B. Miles, Maggie's brother
C. Galen of the First House of Shapeshifters
D. Gavin, one of Sylvia's henchmen
E. An unnamed nobleman

ANSWER: B

Sylvia punishes Miles when they arrive in the Dark Kingdom and has Gavin, a 'shifter falcon, change him. Sylvia then casts a spell on Miles so that he can't return to human form until the leather band is removed from his ankle. Miles returns to human form at the end of *Black Dawn*, but he will forever be a shapeshifter.

Why does Angel lure Gillian into the woods with the sound of a crying child at the beginning of *Dark Angel*?

- A. Angel is lonely.
- B. An injured animal needs rescuing.
- C. Angel wants to show Gillian something frozen in the ice.
- D. A member of Circle Daybreak is waiting there to tell Gillian about her heritage.
- E. Angel is playing a prank.

ANSWER: A

Caught between Earth and the Other Side, Angel is stuck in the between-place. He is lonely and desperate for company. So he lures Gillian into the woods and orchestrates her accident on the ice. But just before Gillian can slip into the Middle Place, Angel reconsiders. Instead of killing Gillian he follows her back to Earth as her spirit rejoins her body. Then Angel devises a plan to take on a physical form by inhabiting David's body.

"Even when we're apart, we'll be looking at the same sky!"

O
h, Ash. He sure knows how to charm a girl! Intense, assertive, and incredibly smart, Ash has a distinctive bad-boy streak. *And* a winning smile. Mary-Lynnette is smitten with Ash and loves how he understands her passion for the night. The electricity between these soulmates is palpable, and these parting words are full of tenderness, if not a little of Ash's signature humor.

Dragons

Dragons are the oldest and most formidable of the shapeshifters, and long predate the first vampire. It is important to remember that dragons are *not* beings who turn themselves into scaly beasts with horns. As with werewolves, these creatures are dragons at their core.

At one point dragons reigned over all of Night World with terror and violence. These immortal beasts were known to breed humans for consumption, much like humans breed cattle. The more human flesh a dragon consumed, it was believed, the more powerful the dragon became. Dragons were put to sleep by the witches more than thirty thousand years ago, and it is said that their blood still runs in the First House of the Shapeshifters.

Dragons dominated the shapeshifters, not just because of their strength, but because dragons have the ability to shift into an infinite number of forms. If a dragon touches any living being, it can assume that figure. Removing a dragon's horns, the seat of a dragon's power, is the only way to prohibit a dragon from changing its appearance and defeat it. Most dragons have one to three horns. But, according to an old parchment kept by the shapeshifters, rare cases of four-horned dragons have been noted. Azhdeha, the dragon in *Witchlight*, broke this record with a remarkable five.

When a dragon changes from its secondary form into its dragon form, it is likened to "a moth being born." A dragon will split his borrowed skin, growing in size and stature to bear a reptilian face and muscular, clawed legs. All dragon fluids release an overpowering sugary odor, and Keller declares that the dragon's battle-torn human skin reeked of such sweetness that it was "an odor to make your stomach lurch."

A dragon's energy is sinister and unassailable. When Keller feels the dragon's mind in the Hallmark store, it is "a core of mindless hatred and evil that seemed to reach back into the mists of time." And this was not even the full force of the dragon's darkness, as he was still in his human shape!

NOTABLE DRAGON

Azhdeha: The first dragon to appear in the Night World series is named Azhdeha. He spends most of his time masquerading in different human forms but reveals his true yellow-green scales at the end of *Witchlight*. Azhdeha claims to have been awakened by a "witch who isn't a witch." With the Old Powers rising and a dragon proclaiming an alliance with the mysterious Night Person who roused him, the threat of other dragons emerging from their sedated slumber is very real. The apocalypse of *Strange Fate* cannot be far behind.

YOU MIGHT BE A DRAGON IF . . .

* you love the Atkins diet and could eat meat at every meal.
* you *really* hate being woken from a deep sleep.
* everyone you know is afraid of you.
* you embrace all types of change.
* you feel a kinship with T. rex.
* sometimes it feels like you've been around since the beginning of time.

In *Huntress*, Hugh mentions that Circle Daybreak discovered an interesting theory about the end of the world. Who came up with the theory and what is it?

ANSWER: According to Hugh, the Hopi Tribe has a theory for the sequence of supremacy among the Night World clans. They believe each clan rules the earth until a natural disaster transitions the authority from one group to another.

The first culture was that of the shapeshifters. They ruled with their animal spirits and were thought of as deities by the humans they governed. During this realm, humans lived in caves and were afraid of what lay beyond. The shapeshifters' society ended when great, fiery volcanoes erupted around the world, changing the weather patterns.

As humans then migrated to different parts of the world, the witches gained control. But after ten thousand years of

domination, there was another shift. This shift was brought on by the Ice Age. The witches fought against the vampires to maintain power but ultimately lost.

The vampires also enjoyed a rule of ten thousand years, until another disaster struck. This time a flood transferred the power into human hands. According to Hugh, this is the current realm. And with humans ruling the earth, the Night People have been lying in wait, anticipating the next evolution of power. Hugh feels the transition is rapidly approaching with the millennium—and that blood and darkness will bring the next succession. The apocalypse is coming. . . .

Thierry promises Hana never to kill again and that he will atone for his sins. Thierry spends centuries doing good deeds and leading Circle Daybreak. Who else must make amends for his past?

A. Ash Redfern
B. John Quinn
C. Galen Drache
D. Todd Akers
E. Chris Grady

ANSWER: A

Bad-boy Ash Redfern knows he has a lot to make up for when he parts company with his soulmate Mary-Lynnette in Briar Creek. He tells her, "I'll fight dragons, just like any knight for his lady. I'll prove myself. You'll be proud of me." And Ash is working to set things right when he meets Hannah at Thierry's mansion. Ash shares his story with Hannah, hoping that his experience—and those of other Daybreakers—will bring her comfort.

What is the "Armageddon of Accessories"?

    A. A bracelet that Iliana admires at the mall

    B. The silver rose ring Thierry gives to Hannah Snow

    C. The brace Prince Delos wears on his arm to protect the Blue Power

    D. A necklace that Blaise designs to destroy Eric

    E. A locket, worn by Jade, that holds her sisters' pictures

ANSWER: D

"With swirls of stars and moons in enchanting patterns," Blaise's unique necklace captivates everyone who sees it. Blaise designs this necklace, like all of her jewelry, to enact a powerful spell—and this one is intended for Eric. In addition to the gems that she incorporates into the design, Blaise laces the necklace with some of Eric's blood, which she lifts from the tissue at the Sun City Animal Hospital.

Whose nickname is Steely Neely?

    A. Aradia
    B. Tanya
    C. Sylvia
    D. Gillian
    E. Maggie

ANSWER: E

Maggie is known as "Steely Neely" by her soccer team. Her brother, Miles, even tells his girlfriend, "Maggie's no rocket scientist, but once she gets hold of something she's just like a little bull terrier." Maggie's remarkable determination saves her brother's life—and that of the Blind Maiden—in *Black Dawn*.

"The five classes would be, from most advanced to most primitive, Animalia, Plantae, Fungi, Protista . . . and Eugene."

W hen Gillian meets Angel, she surrenders her will and independence in exchange for a chance to be popular. Gillian's creative take on the five classes of living creatures comes at the expense of Eugene, Gillian's best friend's boyfriend. Gillian craves popularity and learns a hard lesson: one doesn't rise in status by cutting down someone else's reputation.

Humans, Vermin, Outsiders

I t's no wonder that the Night People want to keep their society secret from humans. Humans are not the most tolerant beings. Not only do they fight among themselves, but humans lash out at those who are not like them, consciously and unconsciously making it their mission to eradicate Night People. Humans are responsible for the Witch Hunts during the Burning Times, tend to be vampire hunters, and rarely react positively to Bigfoot sightings.

Humans don't have supernatural powers, but their kind have taken charge of the world for the past ten thousand years. With the apocalypse on its way, the Night World is looking to unseat the humans' power and regain control. It is the radically divergent beliefs of the Night World and humankind that will bring about a great clash of blood and darkness.

But despite the extremes of thought, humans can also demonstrate great compassion and empathy—for their fellow humans and for those in the Night World. Many humans become ardent supporters of Night World when they learn of its existence. And many humans, still unaware of its reality, practice tolerance and kindness in every facet of their lives.

NOTABLE HUMANS

Mary-Lynnette Carter: Mary-Lynnette is smart, spunky, and a little nosy. Mary-Lynnette is protective of those she loves—including her sensitive brother, Mark, and elderly neighbor, Opal Burdock. Mary-Lynnette contemplates becoming a vampire to be closer to her soulmate—and so that she can better view the stars.

Eric Ross: Eric loves animals and wants to study to become a vet. He is very patient with Roz, his outspoken little sister, and his charm completely captivates Thea. Thea believes him to be "tender but intense. Brave. Profoundly insightful. Shy but with a wicked sense of humor." Aside from not being part of the Night World, Eric is the perfect guy.

Claire Goddard: Jez's human cousin, Claire is prim and prissy, and a miniature of her mother, Nanami. Claire is ignorant of the Night World until she follows Jez to the BART station, where they are both attacked by werewolves. Claire is shocked to learn about the Night

World but becomes astonishingly protective and supportive of her cousin. Claire is also suspected of carrying the Blue Flame.

Maggie Neely: Strong, bold, determined, Maggie Neely is a born organizer. Maggie has a will of steel but a heart of gold. She stands up for herself—and for those who cannot stand up for themselves. Maggie treats everyone she encounters with respect, which in turn earns her great devotion. Maggie is not one to take shortcuts—and she refuses to be changed into a vampire when the possibility presents itself as the easy way out of a tough situation.

YOU MIGHT BE A HUMAN IF . . .

* you think all vampires turn into bats and all witches wear black capes.
* you've heard Night World is a theme park like Disney World.
* you believe werewolves are humans that turn into wolves at the full moon.
* you know casting is for fishing rods and that spelling involves the arrangement of letters to form words.
* you think the place to start looking for other life-forms is on another planet.
* you think the only person who could suck the life out of you is an annoying teacher.

To which clan did Sylvia show her allegiance?

ANSWER: In *Black Dawn* Sylvia declares, "I may be a spell-caster, but I'm not a witch anymore." Raised in the witch tradition by her parents, Sylvia is 100 percent witch but only half Harman. Sylvia's link to this reigning family of Hearth-Women is through her father. But as witches are a matriarchal society, names are passed from a mother to her children—making Sylvia part of the less influential Weald family.

So why does Sylvia denounce her clan? Sylvia has ambitions of becoming part of the Witch Council in Night World, but her birthright keeps her from joining. It angers Sylvia to see other witches—especially half-*human* witches—superseding her with their matrilineal ties to the Harmans.

As a result, Sylvia pledges her loyalty to Hunter Redfern in an attempt to secure a place of power in the new order. Sylvia believes the vampires will rule in the millennium and expects Hunter will serve as the head of the Elders. Unfortunately for Sylvia, Hunter is even more power hungry than she is. When Sylvia is compelled by Aradia and the voice of Hellewise to remove the spell from Prince Delos's arm, she does and then is staked at Hunter's command.

BONUS: Which influential witch is not a descendent of Hellewise through her mother's line?

ANSWER: Aradia, Maiden of the Witches

Who was Angel?

A. David Blackburn
B. A demon
C. Iliana Harman
D. The Welcomer to the Other Side
E. Gary Fargeon

ANSWER: E

Angel is the ghost of Gary Fargeon, who is both a descendent of the witch Emmeth Harman and Gillian's cousin. Gary is a lost witch until members of Circle Daybreak find him and share news of his ancestry. Eager to become powerful, Gary practices his spells in the woods. But Gary commits a terrible crime while working a fire elemental spell. And not long after, he dies in a car crash. Gary's unfinished business on Earth lands him in the Middle Place.

Jeremy isn't the person Mary-Lynnette thinks he is. How does Mary-Lynnette protect herself, and Ash, against Jeremy's attack?

A. With a silver bullet
B. Using self-defense skills she learned at the YWCA
C. With fire
D. With a silver fruit knife
E. By biting him when he is distracted

ANSWER: D

Jeremy Lovett is a werewolf—and a very territorial outlaw werewolf at that. He kills Mrs. B and one of her goats to send a message that the vampires should leave his hunting grounds. Jeremy is also determined to keep Mary-Lynnette from being seduced by Ash. When Jeremy turns against her, Mary-Lynnette runs to her car to retrieve the knife she borrowed from Mrs. B when her station wagon's gas cap was rusted shut. With the ornate silver fruit knife as a weapon, Mary-Lynnette confronts Jeremy.

When Poppy arrives in Las Vegas, she is hungry. Really hungry. Who does she feed on?

A. Ash Redfern
B. James Rasmussen
C. Thea Harman
D. Phillip North
E. Blaise Harman

ANSWER: C

Poppy feeds right after James and Phillip unearth her from her grave, but by the time she arrives in Vegas, it has been almost a full day since she has eaten. Human food doesn't provide the sustenance that she needs, and Poppy is worried she will go into bloodlust, attacking whomever or whatever is nearby. Luckily, Ash takes Poppy to meet his cousins Thea and Blaise. When Thea notices how weak and pale Poppy looks, she offers to be a donor.

"If we do that, then we are the enemy."

When Keller suggests kidnapping Iliana to protect her from the dragon and Night People, Grandma Harman quietly responds with this line. Grandma Harman doesn't need to be loud to be assertive. This old Crone's authority derives from years of leading the witches with wisdom and courage. As she explains, the leaders of Circle Daybreak decided early on that "if we can't convince a Wild Power by reasoning, we will not resort to force. So your orders are to take your team and stay with this child and protect her as long as you can." Those who fight for the daylight won't submit to the tactics of the darkness.

Old Souls

An Old Soul is a human who lives and dies, then comes back as a new person in another time and place. No one in the Night World quite understands how one becomes an Old Soul, but it is believed that vampires cannot be Old Souls, as they don't technically have spirits.

Old Souls tend to follow a similar cycle in each of their lives. But while a pattern of familiar experiences may elicit déjà vu, Old Souls rarely remember their previous incarnation—what they did, who they met. These souls may have been persecuted in one of their lives, nevertheless they do not return to settle old debts or right wrongs. Old Souls are usually very tolerant, as they have experienced lives as people of other races, other creeds, and the opposite sex. The underlying expectation is that even if an Old Soul "perfects" a life, they still reincarnate. The damage an Old Soul has endured during its last lifetime determines when the soul will next awaken. Sometimes it requires only a short period of rest; other times it takes an era.

When an Old Soul returns to Earth, he or she may have characteristics of the person she was in her original life. The new body may have a similar name or hairstyle or hobbies, which helps make it recognizable to those members of the Night World who have lived for centuries. The essence of an Old Soul is always the same: the spirit does not change.

It's not unusual for Old Souls to have Old Soul friends who reincarnate with them. Many times the relationship between these spirits is preserved, though karmic shifts can cause a mother and daughter to reincarnate as father and son or teacher and pupil. Although it is assumed that Old Souls comprise a small portion of the human population, it is impossible to know how many Old Souls exist.

NOTABLE OLD SOULS

Hannah Snow: Hannah Snow is probably the most famous Old Soul in the Night World series. She first meets Thierry, her soulmate, in the first lifetime she remembers, when she is Hana of Three Rivers during the Stone Age. The story of her awakening to her memories is recounted in *Soulmate*.

Hugh Davis: Jez's friend in *Huntress*, Hugh has fair hair and a slight limp from a 'wolf attack. Hugh is unusual, as he is a *fully wakened* Old Soul. Not only can he remember his past lives, but he comes back smarter and more in touch with his consciousness each time he reincarnates.

Iona Skelton: In *Huntress*, eight-year-old Iona is saved from a burning house by a flash of Blue Fire. Mistaken for a Wild Power, Iona has mature-beyond-her-years composure and serenity that reveal she is an Old Soul.

YOU MIGHT BE AN OLD SOUL IF . . .

* you're writing your memoir—and you're already on volume fifty-two.
* you have a keen sense of déjà vu.
* you don't get upset when someone says, "Not in this lifetime!" because you know there will be another.
* you are wise beyond your years.
* you truly believe that practice makes perfect.
* you feel sorry that cats have *only* nine lives.

When Keller finds her soulmate, why does she reject him?

ANSWER: Keller, whose parent abandons her as a child, is reluctant to trust anyone with her heart. She is always guarded, both physically and emotionally. "Love is weakness," she tells her soulmate with bitterness, hoping it will convince him to keep his distance. But her soulmate is persistent. And tender. He wants nothing more than to comfort and protect Keller. But she doesn't want anyone to care for her, as she is sure she will eventually be disappointed. She reasons that any love the two of them could share would be forbidden love, because Keller feels an electric connection with Galen of the First House of Shapeshifters. Not only is he considered the royalty of the 'shifters, he is also betrothed to the Witch Child. His union with Iliana is predicted to join the shapeshifters and the witches. And Keller knows that getting in the way would be like helping the night rule the day.

Hana of Three Rivers is an Old Soul.
Which of the following is *not* a life she lived?

A. Annette of Quebec
B. Ha-nahkt from the Kingdom of Two Lands
C. Anne of St. James Place
D. Hannah Snow of Montana
E. Anora of Honor

ANSWER: C

Meaning "favored grace," Hana and the related Ha-nahkt and Hannah are all lives in which Thierry and Hana are destined to be together—and fated to be apart. Hana also lives as Annette of Quebec, and she remembers living as a slave, a warrior, and even a princess. Her other past names include Hanje, Anora, Xiana, Nan Naiane, Honni, and Ian.

What saves Jez's life after she is staked in *Huntress*?

    A. The silver cord that connects her to Morgead

    B. Claire's Blue Fire

    C. An incantation uttered by a Circle Daybreak nurse

    D. A balm of dried black iris and Morgead's tears

    E. Hugh's powers as an Old Soul

ANSWER: A

Jez is staked by the werewolf Azarius, but she doesn't use her Blue Fire power to save herself. The Blue Flame bursts forth when Pierce is preparing to stake Morgead. Jez loves Morgead and wants to protect him. Lily Redfern, Pierce Holt, and Azarius are vaporized in the fire, and Jez is left on the cusp of death. The cord that connects her heart to Morgead's allows Jez to pull herself back to life.

Rashel first feels compassion for Quinn when

A. Quinn advocates for his vampire friends to be spared at his expense.

B. Quinn recognizes and praises Rashel's honor.

C. Rashel sees Quinn's handsome chiseled face and is overwhelmed by his good looks.

D. the sound of Quinn's voice captivates her and brings her into a hypnotic state.

E. Rashel detects that she and Quinn share a mutual love of Japanese weaponry.

ANSWER: B

Rashel's heart cannot be bought with chocolates or roses. Rashel is a fierce fighter who admires the strength, cunning, and determination that skilled warriors exhibit. She also feels bound by a code of honor. Quinn understands this, and it makes Rashel respect Quinn. While they are enemies, they approach each other as equals—which brings out Rashel's compassionate side.

"*When* will they learn that witches never wore pointy hats?"

B laise is the cousin inclined toward emotional spontaneous combustion, but Thea is the one who gets angry when she learns the human students at her new high school are planning a witch-themed Halloween party. Given the witch mannequins dressed in ridiculous clothing and displayed in torture devices, is it any wonder that Thea thinks humans aren't very smart or understanding?

KNOW YOUR LINGO

"The night has a thousand eyes." You answer with which of the following statements:

    A. "But love is blind."
    B. "And the day only one."
    C. "Tread carefully, for you are being watched."
    D. "Heed the call of darkness."
    E. "Watch carefully for falling stars."

ANSWER: B

If you want to attend a meeting of the Lancers, you need to know the secret code. Rashel knows what to say into the intercom to be buzzed up to the hideout. The response that comes from Eliot is "And the day only one." In this context, the line speaks to the number of conniving vampires who are stalking humans and the individual vampire hunters (who work alone to avoid detection) protecting the Outsider society.

BONUS: What is this line from?

ANSWER: A poem by Francis William Bourdillon. Hugh references the poem in regard to the Wild Power prophecy in *Huntress*.

What Is Your Clan?

A re you part of the Night World? Would you hang out with the Harmans or vacation with a pack of werewolves? Find out with this quiz! Circle your responses to the following questions, then match your answers with the key on page 178 to find your clan.

1. It's Valentine's Day and your soulmate bought you flowers! What kind of blooms are in the arrangement?

A. Black iris, maybe even some black roses

B. Black foxglove

C. Black dahlia

D. Black dragon's blood sedum

E. Yuck. Why send black flowers? You expect your bouquet to be pink and red and white.

2. What kind of car do you drive?

A. It isn't the finest car in the parking lot, but your old station wagon is reliable . . . until the engine catches fire. But you know people with cars (like Fords) and even some with really cool cars (like BMW convertibles), and they can give you a ride.

B. A black Acura Integra

C. You usually carpool with friends, so it depends on who is driving.

D. You don't have a car and, though it takes a little longer to get places, you like to walk. If there is somewhere you need to be in a hurry, you're a strong runner.

E. A Geo or a Lincoln Continental

3. You are working on a mixed-media project for shop class. Which material *won't* you be using?

A. Iron
B. It doesn't really matter. You'll make do with whatever is available.
C. Silver
D. Wood
E. You like to keep your aesthetic decisions to yourself. Sorry.

4. **You are smitten. What first attracted you to your crush?**

A. It's a yin-and-yang connection: you complement each other.

B. A vast knowledge of deities—and the respect shown for his/her mother

C. That delicate place on the neck, just below the ear . . .

D. A sense of humor

E. A good heart

5. **What's your favorite holiday/occasion?**
   A. Lunar eclipses
   B. It changes from year to year.
   C. Aren't birthdays great?
   D. The solstices—both winter and spring
   E. Spring equinox or any day when you can
      honor your family and your heritage

6. What are puppies?

A. Werewolves

B. Your cousins

C. Mammals whose saliva has many practical applications

D. Potentially your alter ego

E. Doggie! I want one! Go fetch, boy!

7. **When you die, what arrangements would you like made?**
   A. Coffin or cremation. It's not like I'll be around
      to know.
   B. Umm . . . I'm not going anywhere. Deal.
   C. It depends on how I go. . . .
   D. No taxidermy—I mean, embalming. Burial is fine.
   E. I don't like fire, so skip the Viking funeral, please.

8. **When it comes to family**

   A. you can trace your lineage back to the Stone Age.

   B. your parents can be really annoying, but you love them.

   C. you are close but never have meals together.

   D. there is nothing else. When you're in, you're in.

   E. it's complicated. Your friends are your family.

SCORE YOUR ANSWERS:

1.
- A. A
- B. B
- C. C
- D. D
- E. E

2.
- A. E
- B. A
- C. D
- D. B
- E. C

3.
- A. C
- B. E
- C. B
- D. A
- E. D

4.
- A. D
- B. C
- C. A
- D. E
- E. B

5.
- A. B
- B. D
- C. E
- D. C
- E. A

6.
- A. A
- B. B
- C. C
- D. D
- E. E

7.
- A. E
- B. A
- C. D
- D. B
- E. C

8.
- A. C
- B. E
- C. B
- D. A
- E. D

Mostly As? You're a lamia. Once a vampire, always a vampire. Dedicated to family and your rich heritage, you have a lot of pride for your clan. You always think you know best and are stubborn to a fault—which probably has something to do with the fact that you're immortal. You're nearly perfect, and you sometimes try to change others so they are more like you.

Mostly Bs? You're a werewolf. You are a 'wolf through and through, but you live a portion of your life in human form. Other sects of the Night World look down on your kind, so you might even say, "It's a dog eat dog world." You may stick close to a pack, but chances are you're a loner and very territorial. The good news? You will always have a thick head of hair.

Mostly Cs? You're a witch. You know the recipe for success and follow it to the letter! You can trace your lineage back to ancient times and celebrate the matriarchs in your family. Sometimes the weight of tradition can be overwhelming, but you are always buoyed by your circle of friends.

Mostly Ds? You're a shapeshifter. Elusive, unpredictable, flexible: your kind tends toward the extreme. Whether you identify as cool and collected or feisty and bold, you are very protective of your friends and family. Call it animal instinct, but you assess the variables of each situation and maneuver with lithe precision.

Mostly Es? You're a human. Night World, what? Oh, come on. You have an overactive imagination. Creatures of the darkness are the things of horror movies and novels. . . . Now let's go to the deli for lunch!

Tie between two choices? Your parents came from different clans and the blood of both races courses through you. You like how this makes you unique, and the other Circle Daybreakers embrace you for who you are.

The Soulmate Principle

The soulmate principle is an accepted truth in the Night World: every person has a perfect match. Not just someone with whom you are compatible, but someone with whom you have an undeniable connection. Although you may not love each other—or even like each other!—initially, it is tangible from the first moment that skin touches skin.

Soulmates share a special telepathic bond that goes beyond the link that some vampires and witches have. This bond is literally mind-bending, allowing each soulmate to see into the other's psyche, heart, and soul. Most soulmates also see a silver cord connecting their two beings. This cord can be stretched, but it is impossible to break. The soulmate connection is stronger than any friendship or family relationship. As

James tells his soulmate, Poppy, "You don't love somebody because of their looks or their clothes or their car. You love them because they sing a song that nobody but you can understand." Hannah Snow believes her soulmate, Thierry, is more than her perfect match. He is "one who was sacred to her, who was the other half of the mysteries of life for her. The one who would always be there for her, helping her, watching her back, picking her up when she fell down, listening to her stories—no matter how many times she told them."

Distance may keep two soulmates apart, but most will eventually find one another. Fate will draw them together. And when that happens, it's electric.

But love, even soulmate love, isn't always easy. Especially if soulmates are of different worlds. In the Night World, falling in love with a human is punishable by death. But as Thea reasoned, "Maybe there was magic stronger than spells. Maybe the soulmate principle was responsible, and if two people were meant to be together, nothing could keep them apart."

What Is Your Soulmate Relationship?

L ooking for your soulmate? Find out what kind of Night World relationship you are destined for by circling your responses to the questions on the following pages. Then match your answers with the key on page 193 to find your soulmate!

1. **You arrive at a party, and**

A. though you and your date arrive together, you circulate separately before meeting up to relax on the couch with friends.

B. say hi to a few friends as you work your way toward the stereo. You're ready to help DJ.

C. smile at everyone like he or she is your best friend. You're always good natured.

D. head outside to see what's going on in the backyard. You can have more in-depth conversations there—and spy on those trying to take advantage of the dark.

E. acknowledge people with a nod, positioning yourself with your back to the wall near a bowl of chips and an exit.

F. hit the center of the dance floor. It's your time to shine!

2. **What's the primary quality you are looking for in a soulmate?**

    A. You are looking for a lot of qualities in a soulmate—now if only you could find them all in one person!

    B. Someone who adds balance to your life

    C. Someone to spar with, intellectually and physically

    D. Someone who will be there for you in times of trouble

    E. Someone with whom to share the night . . .

    F. Someone who recognizes the real you

3. Which famous fictional couple do you admire most?

A. Romeo and Juliet from guess which
Shakespearean play?

B. Holden Caulfield and girls in J.D. Salinger's
The Catcher in the Rye

C. Mr. Darcy and Elizabeth Bennet from Jane Austen's
Pride and Prejudice

D. Mowgli and Shanti in the Disney version of Rudyard
Kipling's *The Jungle Book*

E. Prince Phillip and Princess Aurora in *Sleeping Beauty*

F. Captain Li Shang and Mulan in the tale *Mulan*

4. You and your soulmate plan an afternoon in the park. What do you take with you?

A. A Frisbee. Maybe even a yoga mat. You are not one to sit still, and like self-discipline. That said: you have a weakness for jelly-stick donuts. You pack those, too.

B. Wild berries you picked near your house and a field guide, so you can identify any rocks or fossils you might find.

C. A few cans of Coke, some trance music for zoning out, a beach umbrella, and two pairs of extra-dark sunglasses.

D. Iced tea, candy corn, and a few magazines. Your soulmate will have already stopped at the gourmet market to pick up everything else you'll need for a picnic.

E. A book of poetry and Stratego. And some Mad Libs.

F. Apricot juice, sparkling water, and a few sandwiches. Don't forget the binoculars for people watching!

5. **If you and your soulmate were to take a dream vacation, where would you go?**

  A. Wherever there's a good view of the next eclipse
  B. Japan
  C. The rainforest
  D. Somewhere exotic, like Egypt or Quebec
  E. Somewhere luxurious: a five-star hotel or maybe a decadent cruise
  F. Las Vegas or the Pacific Northwest

6. You're getting ready for the first dance of the school year. What will you wear?

A. You like form-fitting clothing and opt for a jumpsuit with a low-cut neckline.

B. Something casual and comfortable. You're there to spend time with your friends, not show off.

C. You plan on pairing dark jeans with a cool leather jacket.

D. You're not sure yet, but most of your wardrobe is black. So you'll be wearing black.

E. A white linen sheath dress with an ornate necklace of beautiful beadwork.

F. A tux with cuff links—you know how to look sharp and stick out in a crowd.

7. Your soulmate knows you better than anyone else and plans a treat just for you. What do you do on your date?

A. You get ice cream, then visit the music store, where you are treated to any two albums you want. Just like before you started dating!

B. You spend the evening outside, watching the sun set and the stars come out . . . and kissing.

C. You expect to go out for an expensive dinner at an exclusive restaurant. And when you get picked up, your date better fork over the car keys 'cause you're driving!

D. You take a private self-defense class together. And then a nice long walk.

E. You so rarely get to spend time together that it is a pleasure simply to be in each other's company. But you still enjoy a lavish evening, spoiled with limos and luxury.

F. You pick out a movie (just in case), and while you have a hard time giving up control, you have a lot of fun when your soulmate takes you to a carnival and wins you prizes.

8. **You and your soulmate have a fight. What do you do?**

A. Your soulmate has a knack for soothing you when you get angry. Calming words and a pressure-point massage are all you need to turn back into your usual self.

B. Fight? You never fight. But if you did, you'd stop holding hands for five minutes. Then you'd promptly make up.

C. You get mad. You yell. You walk away. But tomorrow is a new day, and it's as if it never happened.

D. After some biting remarks, you stop shouting—and realize that you both had valid points. You agree to disagree.

E. While you are tempted to pull the silent treatment, you decide to be the bigger person and start a conversation.

F. You like getting mad. And your soulmate is going to need to apologize first. No one is going to coax an "I'm sorry" out of you.

9. **How would you best describe your soulmate's relationship with your family?**

    A. Your family is gone, but your soulmate helps you pay tribute to them.

    B. You haven't had time to introduce them yet, but you think they will get along.

    C. Sometimes it gets tense when everyone is together, but that's only because your family doesn't know your soulmate well enough yet.

    D. Your soulmate believes you are the most wonderful member of the family and has eyes only for you. And it had better stay that way.

    E. Your soulmate *is* your family.

    F. Your soulmate immediately charmed your family.

1. A. F
B. A
C. E
D. B
E. D
F. C

2. A. C
B. F
C. D
D. A
E. B
F. E

3. A. E
B. C
C. B
D. F
E. A
F. D

4. A. D
B. E
C. A
D. C
E. F
F. B

5. A. B
B. D
C. F
D. E
E. C
F. A

6. A. F
B. B
C. A
D. D
E. E
F. C

7. A. A
B. B
C. C
D. D
E. E
F. F

8. A. F
B. A
C. E
D. B
E. D
F. C

9. A. D
B. E
C. A
D. C
E. F
F. B

Mostly As? You have a Poppy/James Soulmate. You are friends long before you realize you are soulmates. And then, all at once, everything changes and nothing changes. There is no one you trust more. And no one you want to be with more. You feel safe when you are together, and you are excited to explore this new stage of friendship.

Mostly Bs? You have a Mary-Lynnette/Ash Soulmate. You and your soulmate are both hotheaded and smart, and have a tendency to involve yourselves in other people's business. You're not always on the same page, but when you both channel your energies into your relationship, your passion burns bright like the midday sun.

Mostly Cs? You have a Blaise/insert-name-of-a-hot-guy-here Soulmate. Okay, okay. So he's not *quite* your soulmate. You're fine with that. You just haven't met your soulmate yet. But that's no reason to sit around moping on the couch. You like to be out and having fun. And if in the meantime there's a little competition about who gets your time and affection, so be it. . . .

Mostly Ds? You have a Rashel/Quinn Soulmate. You're serious about everything you do, and your relationship is no exception. Discipline and reserve are an integral part of who you are, though some might perceive you as being cold and distant. Lucky for you, your soulmate agrees that these qualities add to the romantic tension.

Mostly Es? You have a Hannah/Thierry Soulmate. You are charming and compassionate, and sometimes others take advantage of your goodwill—but not your soulmate. Your soulmate is determined to do right by you, even though you've had a few bumps in the road. Together you look toward the future, not toward the past.

Mostly Fs? You have a Keller/Galen Soulmate. You and your soulmate are proof that opposites do attract. Two more different people couldn't be found, but you complement each other. If it benefits your relationship, you are willing to change so that you can grow together.

The Prophecy

Four to stand between the light and the shadow,
Four of blue fire, power in their blood.
Born in the year of the blind Maiden's vision;
Four less one and darkness triumphs.

Four Wild Powers have been sent to combat the impending apocalypse. Each commands Blue Fire, which is the most powerful of the rainbow of witchlight colors and can conquer even the mightiest spell or beast. But to access the Blue Fire, Wild Powers must summon all of their strength and give of themselves—they must let their own blood flow.

The prophecy states that the Wild Powers were all born in the same year, before Aradia, Maiden of the Witches, lost her sight. That means that the Wild Powers are now seventeen years old and preparing not to take their SATs, but to fight against the end of the world. It is a fight that will require the utmost determination and cooperation. Should even one Wild Power change allegiance or fall, the cause will be lost. . . .

The vampires eagerly await the end of the humans' reign. They are bloodthirsty and believe the apocalypse will bring them back to power. But they are the only clan remaining under the Night World banner. Of the witches, all but the darkest spellcasters in Circle Midnight have seceded. The Dark Ninjas, a group of stealth vampires and shapeshifters, are eager to fight on behalf of the evil faction of Night World, but will their alliance be strong enough?

Circle Daybreak is summoning all of the support they can to challenge the darkness. Their Circle is growing. Yet, amid the turmoil, the humans are unaware that the Old Powers are rising and that the greatest power struggle of all time is about to commence.

Circle Daybreak

One of the original circles of witches, Circle Daybreak is founded at a time when witches would take human husbands to compensate for the small male-witch population. The Circle embraced inter-race unions and taught magic to humans.

Revived by Lord Thierry as a means to atone for his wrongdoings during the Stone Age, Circle Daybreak is an underground community in modern Night World. Couples composed of a Night Person and a human find refuge and support from Circle Daybreak, and the rise of the soulmate principle brings increased relevance and importance to this group.

As the time of darkness approaches, Circle Daybreak grows in size and purpose. Circle Daybreakers are committed to locating and protecting the four Wild Powers. They believe that Night People and humans can coexist peacefully, and the Circle becomes its own political faction within the Night World. The witches officially secede from the Night World Council in *Black Dawn*, aligning with Circle Daybreak. When the witches and shapeshifters form a partnership in *Witchlight*, the 'shifters also lend their support to Circle Daybreak.

The remaining evil Night World powers, the vampires and the darkest of the witches, still have great influence. And with Circle Daybreak and the sinister forces on the Night World Council both clamoring to locate the last Wild Power, the fate of the world hangs in the balance.

The Wild Powers

One from the land of kings long forgotten;
One from the hearth which still holds the spark;
One from the Day World where two eyes are watching;
One from the twilight to be one with the dark.

ONE FROM THE LAND OF KINGS
LONG FORGOTTEN

Prince of the Dark Kingdom, Delos is a vampire with the power of the Blue Fire. From the time he was a small child, this Redfern is groomed to use his blue energy at his father's request. Delos's golden eyes are mesmerizing—but full of sorrow. "Treated as a weapon from the time he was born," Delos is most understanding of the gift and curse that it is to be a Wild Power. Delos breaks ties with his family, his past, and the brace that restrains his Blue Fire to decide his own future.

Persuaded to follow his heart by his soulmate, Maggie, Delos's greatest desire is to exceed his father's expectations. Delos decides to govern the vampires at Black Dawn not with an iron fist, but with a strong hand. Maggie helps Delos see that he does not need to change who he is in the face of adversity; if he stays true to himself, the necessary power will come from within.

ONE FROM THE HEARTH WHICH STILL HOLDS THE SPARK

Iliana Harman is the prophesied Witch Child. The witches foretell of the Witch Child unifying the witches and the shapeshifters through marriage. Shapeshifters would then join the witches as part of Circle Daybreak, strengthening the Circle for the impending battle against the darkness. Witches waited centuries for the Witch Child's arrival, though it is unclear if the shapeshifters anticipated her coming with the same enthusiasm.

As with most of the other Wild Powers, Iliana is unaware of her ability to summon the Blue Fire. In fact, Iliana is completely *unaware* of Night World and her place in it until she is ambushed by a dragon and Keller at the Hallmark store in the mall.

Iliana is pure, delicate even, which, as Winnie in *Witchlight* asserts, is "not the same as being *chicken*." Iliana has an overwhelmingly good spirit, and her genuine interest and concern for others make her well loved by all. She radiates inner joy, and others find it peaceful to be around her, making Iliana extremely popular at her high school. Her pale blond hair and violet eyes captivate the boys, but those familiar with the Night World know they are Harman traits. And like her ancestor Hellewise, Illiana is both courageous and unselfish, winning the respect of even the most critical Circle Daybreaker, Rashka Keller.

Iliana is able to summon the power of the ages, turning her witchlight into Blue Power when fighting Azhdeha.

ONE FROM THE DAY WORLD
WHERE TWO EYES ARE WATCHING

With red, flowing hair, a quick temper, and a charismatic personality, Jez's place in the Redfern family tree is undeniable. But when a secret from Jez's past creeps into her present, she must reevaluate all that she knows . . . and leave the Night World behind.

Jez is half-human, a vermin like those she has spent her life hunting for amusement. With a new understanding of her lineage, Jez leaves her life as Huntress to defend and protect humans against the violence of Night World.

But as the Old Powers begin to rise, a flash of Blue Fire is recorded on a newsreel: one of the four Wild Powers lives in Jez's old haunts. Eager to help Circle Daybreak, Jez Redfern returns to challenge the new vampire gang leader—and to search out the Wild Power. Jez seamlessly infiltrates her old gang, but she soon discovers that she must rely on her human wit if she is to masquerade as a vampire.

As half-human and half-vampire, Jez is the first of her kind. When she doesn't use her vampire powers, she has no need to feed on mortal blood. And as a human, she is not susceptible to vampire weaknesses. With the sun watching from the human world and the moon watching from the Night World, Jez discovers she is the half-breed Wild Power sent to protect the world from blood and darkness. And, being Jez, she naturally assumes she will lead the way.

ONE FROM THE TWILIGHT TO BE
ONE WITH THE DARK . . .

The full meaning of the prophecy has yet to be understood. Secrets will be revealed, new truths will come to light, and a different kind of power will cause all the prophecies, ancient and modern, to be reconsidered. . . .

Night World Nostalgia

Y ou might remember stumbling upon *Secret Vampire* in the bookstore. Or possibly waiting with anticipation for *The Chosen* or *Black Dawn* to publish, or carrying a stack of four or five Night World books home from the library. Maybe you still have all nine titles on your bookshelves. Perhaps one dog-eared book even sits on your nightstand right now.

Night World has captivated readers since the books' original publication in the late 1990s. The series got a makeover in June 2008, but no companion guide would be complete without the first-edition covers!

Secret Vampire, June 1996

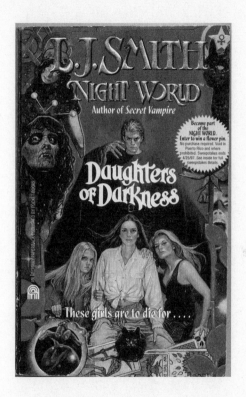

Daughters of Darkness, August 1996

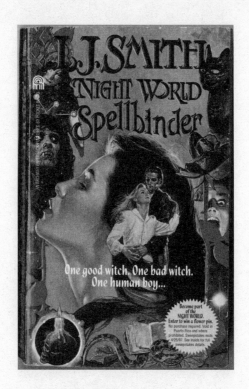

Spellbinder, October 1996

Dark Angel, December 1996

The Chosen, February 1997

Soulmate, April 1997

Huntress, September 1997

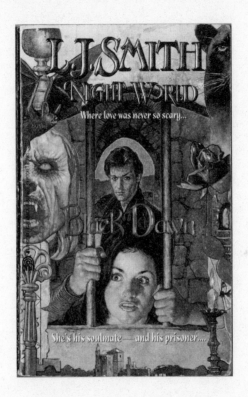

Black Dawn, November 1997

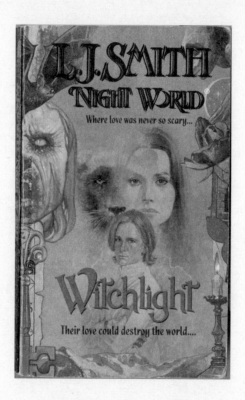

Witchlight, January 1998

25 Facts About L.J. Smith

1. My favorite flowers are Black Magic roses.
2. I am addicted to roller coasters.
3. When I was ten, I wanted to be a nun.
4. For most of my life my hair has been long enough to sit on.
5. I grew to my full height of 5'4½" by the time I was in sixth grade.
6. My favorite state is Hawaii (favorite island: Maui).
7. I have fainted three times in my life.
8. I want to get a tattoo. (A Japanese kanji that means "power." I think it might give me some.)
9. My sister calls me Bunny.
10. I am very bad at multiplication.

11. My favorite holiday is Halloween.

12. I think we can all learn a lesson from *Yertle the Turtle*.

13. I have a phantom cat that jumps on my bed at night.

14. My junior high friends and I once TP-ed an entire school.

15. I am violently allergic to strawberries.

16. I successfully performed the Heimlich maneuver on my nephew.

17. I enjoy earthquakes.

18. In a Scottish castle I *think* I saw the ghost of a child.

19. I can wiggle my nose.

20. Quantum physics is a passion of mine.

21. I have gotten two traffic tickets in my life.

22. I have cold feet at night.

23. I love sushi with just a *touch* of wasabi mustard.

24. I scream at the sight of a cricket.

25. I once got a fortune-telling card saying I would marry a prince. Where is he?

L.J. Smith and the Night World—Revealed!

First L.J. Smith wrote the Night World books, and then you wrote to her. Over the years, Lisa has received and responded to countless letters and e-mails. And now she has chosen ten of the most interesting, most frequently asked questions—and answered them. Entertaining and candid, it's Lisa and the Night World up close and personal!

When did you begin to write?
When did you decide to be a writer?

People often ask this, and all I can say is I was making up stories before I could read. Unlike authors who were prodigies, I didn't learn to read until I was taught in first grade, but I certainly knew how to make up a story. Whenever I saw something on TV or heard a story, I would keep making up what would happen next, or what I would do if I were in the story. I would also make up stories about exciting things that happened to me or about interesting people I met. Maya is probably an amalgamation of all the babysitters I hated!

The book I recall most clearly from my childhood (before I started school) is the wonderful *D'Aulaires' Book of Greek Myths*. I particularly adored the story of how Persephone, a young girl, was innocently gathering flowers when Hades, dressed all in black and riding in a black chariot with black horses, suddenly burst out of the ground and carried her away to his dark realm under the earth. I loved to hear how Persephone was doomed to spend six months of each year in the dark underground because she ate six pomegranate seeds while there. But

I wouldn't have eaten those pomegranate seeds! I would have tricked Hades by *pretending* to eat them and then spitting them out.

Thinking back on this story, I wonder if, as young as I was, I had some concept of the archetypical Gothic tale of the beautiful young girl being wooed and pursued by the dark, seemingly all-powerful lover. It could be that I was in training for writing about vampires even then. But one thing is certain. I can't remember a time when I didn't want to be a writer.

When do you like to write?

I like best to write in the morning when I first wake up, before even having a cup of coffee. I run to the computer (if I haven't fallen asleep on it) and just dash off a few pages without thinking about how to edit them. This helps turn off the little censor inside my head; the one that choked me up for ten years and that is telling me right now that this is not a very good sentence. Writing at breakneck speed before I do anything else seems to start the motor of my imagination.

The real question isn't when I like to write—ever since I decided to become a full-time author, it has been a job that requires me to write morning, noon, and night—but when and where I work out thorny, plot problems.

That's when I have to walk. Ideally, I walk on the long, sparsely populated beaches in Point Reyes National Seashore. But if I'm not at my cabin, I have to take to the road, walking with my headphones blaring my favorite music into my ears. If neither of these are possible (say, it's after midnight and I don't fancy being alone on the side-walk), I used to drive the freeway with the stereo blaring. Now I'm more environmentally conscious. So when I need to create and I can't get outside and I don't have a houseguest—please don't think I'm crazy—I turn up the music and walk very briskly *inside* the house. And I actually act out my story, being all the characters in turn. I've done this . . . well, forever. Since I was a kid.

It doesn't absolutely require the music, but that really helps.

You've written a bit about how you get inspired—what do you like about being a writer? What keeps you writing?

It's really not a question of what keeps me writing. It's how to stop it once it starts. I love the storytelling machine in my head, but it is run completely by my unconscious. Once it stopped dead for ten years, leaving me staring at blank computer screens, notebooks, napkins, receipt backs—all the things I used to need to scribble down my thoughts. Then, a few years ago, it began to chug like the Little Engine That Could and then it began to spin in overdrive. Once again I find myself squinting at napkins, staring at my really, really horrible handwriting, and asking friends, "Did I say anything to you about a goose story? A gross—no, ghost story—and a ghastly spaniel? A sparrow? Oh, a *specter*!"

Because that's the other thing I make use of when writing: friends and family. Know me long enough and I'm certain to start asking, "So I want to write about how Jez and Morgead first met, but I need a reason for them to fight . . ." Or, "Dad, what's the best thing a quarterback can do to win a game?" Back in the days before the Internet, I asked my hairdresser, who was also a terrific mechanic, "If you're building a car, what's something awful that someone can accidentally do to it?" I got answers to all three and the last two are in stories or books. At first, people often just stare at me until I start brainstorming, saying anything that comes into my head. Usually after a few minutes of this, they start to play along, and somehow the problem gets solved and the storytelling machine whizzes off with me in hot pursuit.

What do I like about being a writer? Everything. For most of my life, it's been how I define myself. I am, therefore I write. Oh, and getting feedback! That's the icing on the cake for me. I write for readers, otherwise it would be much easier to keep my stories in my head. When a reader says, "I never really liked to read until I found your books," it's like champagne. When a reader says, "Your books got me through high school," it makes me want to cry and do the Happy Dance all at once. When a reader says, "I read your books and now I'm a teacher or a writer myself," it's almost too much for me to take in.

But even the simplest e-mail makes me feel humble. I'm just doing what I have to do, and if it helps other people in any way, giving them a few hours of enjoyment, I'm happy. Very, very happy.

How did you create the intricate backstory in Night World? Did you start from the beginning and write to the end, or did you have a plan from the start?

Both, really. I had to have a game plan from the start because there were so many rules and traditions for the vampires. The Night World has rules about humans: they are never to reveal the Night World to a human and never fall in love with one. Lamia vampires traditionally name their children after a plant, animal, or mineral (resulting in names like Rowan, Kestrel, and Jade, from *Daughters of Darkness*). There *are* two kinds of vampires, lamia and made vampires. No one older than nineteen can be made into a vampire at all—after that the body doesn't have the physical flexibility to change and simply burns out. I introduce things like that in *Secret Vampire* as a sort of gentle prelude to the more complicated backstory that comes in later books.

Then I introduce Hunter Redfern and his descendents in *Daughters of Darkness*, and I explain Hunter's history and the kinship ceremony with the witch Maeve Harman. Later, in *Spellbinder*, I add another piece of the puzzle, about how both the Redferns and the Harmans go back to Hecate Witch-Queen and her two very dissimilar daughters, Maya and Hellewise. Maya has a lamia son, Red Fern, and of course he is the origin of all the Redferns. Hellewise has a daughter, from whom all the witches are descended. "Daughter of Hellewise" *means* witch.

So I had the background in my head, and I tried to dole it out in little pieces so it wouldn't sound too much like a history lesson. But Night World history changed radically when I introduced new prophecies about the end of the world in *Huntress* and *Black Dawn* and *Witchlight*. And it isn't until *Witchlight* that I unveil the means by which the world will be destroyed. The means actually scared even me, they were so merciless. And that's how dragons entered the Night World.

How do you keep track of all of the Night World characters and lore?

On paper. It's the only way. Otherwise I could never remember that Jez Redfern is related to Thea Harman. She's Thea's seventeenth cousin once removed. (Lamia and witches are related through Hunter Redfern and Maeve Harman, remember? They had a daughter: Roseclear. . . .)

I got a family tree software package, and laboriously, I filled it in, name by name, marriage by marriage, child by child, until I had a set of ancient Harmans and Redferns, a set of Pilgrim's Age Harmans and Redferns (this was important for the kinship ceremony and for the introduction of Quinn and Hunter's three lamia daughters), and a very large set of modern Harmans and Redferns.

When I printed it out, on about a zillion pieces of letter-size paper, it covered the floor like a five-foot-by-five-foot carpet. It even included dates of marriages and "occupations": lamia, made vampire, witch, psychic, human, etc. I taped it together to make a giant poster, and I made a new chart with each book. They were works of art that eventually got so huge and unwieldy as I continued to add new soulmates that I finally gave up. (I think my cat mistook a newly made poster for a litter box and that also had something to do with it). But I still have most of the information.

The same with the prophecies. I keep them all in a special file and add each as it comes along—otherwise I'd forget all of them.

If you were part of the Night World, which clan would you want to be part of?

I would love to be a witch. I would marry a vampire, and he would love me so much that he would stop being a humanitarian and become a simple carnivore, biting deer or cows and only taking enough blood as is necessary to live on, because naturally we would be part of Circle Daybreak. I would let him bite *me* only on special occasions, like his birthday. Or holidays. Or every day—but just a little. Like every couple in which one partner is a vampire, we would walk that thin line between the thrill of joining minds and the danger of changing the other partner.

We would be soulmates, and we probably would have had a rocky courtship: he would be a Redfern, with a Redfern's typical arrogance and power. However, I would be firm but gentle with him—something like taming a big dog—and we would be so drawn together by the silver cord that we would hardly be able to stand being out of each other's sight.

I would definitely want to be a Harman—a direct descendent of

Hellewise Hearth-Woman. That would make practically all of the characters in my books my cousin, more or less distant. I would originally belong to Circle Twilight, like Thea in *Spellbinder*, but I would *always* use my powers for good. My witchlight would be so hot and powerful that it burned blue, like the bottom of a flame. That would allow me to heal people's wounds and diseases.

I might even go on a sort of pilgrimage, traveling from hospital to hospital, healing the sickest patients without them ever knowing I was doing it. I would heal and heal until finally I fainted (gracefully) with exhaustion, and my soulmate would catch me and gently carry me back to our car. Then I would rest against his shoulder until I woke up and was ready to begin the crusade all over again.

My husband could spend a lot of his time fighting off the assassins that the Vampire Council or the Circle Midnight (*wicked!*) witches would undoubtedly send after me. He'd enjoy that.

Who is your favorite character from the Night World? Why?

Out of the books already published? I'm going to have to say it's . . . Jez Redfern from *Huntress*. I love writing about Jez because she's so impulsive and unpredictable; she might do anything at any moment. She thinks with her heart—and her snakewood fighting stick.

Jez is dealt a tough hand. She's actually the first vampire-human hybrid. Her father is one of the lamia, the born vampires, the family vampires, but her mother is human. Vampires find out that Jez's parents broke Night World law and kill them both. Jez is four years old and survives this savage attack, but her memory doesn't. She grows up thinking of herself as a vampire. But when her memories are triggered and come rushing back to engulf her, she doesn't collapse, or become catatonic, or try to forget. Jez switches sides and begins to *defend* humans from vampires.

Jez is intelligent and a natural leader, but by no means perfect. She has a quick temper and is always getting into fights with Morgead, her soulmate. They trade the leadership of their vampire gang back and forth as they challenge each other for the title. It's fun to write about their wrangling, and equally fun to write about their making up.

I enjoy the energy that Jez brings to any scene because she is sure to start an argument, jump on a table, or somehow capture the attention of the audience. She certainly doesn't believe that women should be soft and fragile and demure.

How do you feel about shapeshifters? The only good one in a lead role is Keller.

For a long while, I couldn't really see the beauty in werewolves and they really get a bad rap in the Night World. They tend to be the thugs, the hired muscle, or insanely territorial and unstable.

But when I wrote *Soulmate*, Lupe comes in her wolf form to rescue Hannah, and I saw shapeshifters in a whole new light. After all, I reasoned, I adored animals, sometimes more than people. So a person turning into an animal doesn't have to be a villain. But I didn't want to focus on a werewolf; everyone was doing werewolves. I'd seen the movie *Cat People* at some point and thought the cats were absolutely gorgeous. So I decided to have a heroine who could turn into a black panther—voluntarily.

That was Keller, and from the very first pages of *Witchlight* she was running everything in her own brusque, apparently invulnerable, way. She was willing to attack a dragon alone. Granted, the dragon was in human form and she herself was a huge beast with jaws that could crack the skull of a water buffalo, but attacking it meant her death and she knew it—but never hesitated. I couldn't help but admire her guts.

Keller is actually one of the most wounded and vulnerable characters in all the Night World stories. She needed a gentle soulmate to soothe her and remind her that she had value as a person. So I created Galen, Prince of the Shapeshifters, to help her learn to love and trust again.

That's how I learned to love shapeshifters. I may even do a werewolf story someday. . . .

If you could be a shapeshifter, what would be your shape and why?

I'm tempted to say a black panther like Keller from *Witchlight*, because black panthers are smooth and silken, and I'm sure that just *moving* must feel wonderful to them. But the truth is I'd rather fly. I've wanted to fly since childhood, and parasailing, while fun, is just not the same thing. I'd like to be a bird large enough so nothing would want to eat me. I'll pass on having to eat roadkill or decaying carcasses, too, thanks. So I guess I'd like to be a peregrine falcon. (For some reason bald eagles just don't ring my bells. Maybe because they remind me of the government.)

By the way, black panthers, falcons, *and* bald eagles are all endangered. I am a member of the World Wildlife Fund and have adopted an animal that I will reveal when *Strange Fate* is published (my bad boy is a shapeshifter and it's a secret). I'm also a member of the Nature Conservancy. Both organizations help endangered species, of which there are an alarming number. This is a cause I really believe in. You can do lots of things that don't require spending money to help conserve the natural world—things like recycling, going to a car wash instead of doing it yourself (really—it conserves more than four hundred gallons of water!), carpooling to school (make new friends!), or just searching online for local agencies where you can take your pick of other ways to help.

But back to being a falcon. I would soar on the wind currents and strike dazzling poses, since bird watchers love to see peregrine falcons. I would search the ground with my falcon-keen eyes and then dive for that mouse and scarf it down, because I'm sure it . . . would . . . taste . . . really . . . yummy. . . .

Maybe I would be the world's first vegetarian falcon.

What about Old Souls? How did you create Hannah and her multiple lives? Can Hannah really remember all her lives?

Hannah was fun to create because I could put her into any time period that interested me, and there were several time periods that were already favorites of mine, like ancient Egypt. I also wanted Thierry to be able to recognize Hannah in each life without her looking exactly the same every time. The easiest way to do that was to create a physical attribute that *wouldn't* change and would be easy to see.

That was how Hannah got her birthmark; but I wanted to make it an almost attractive birthmark, and so I always describe it as looking as if it had been traced on her cheekbone. What really was traced on her cheek was *blood*, and this soulmate had a whopper of a crime to atone for: the death of Hannah's entire kin group back in cave-dweller days—and the death of Hannah herself.

But Thierry also has extenuating circumstances, and millennia (not just centuries!) to spend doing good deeds. He develops an air of ancient sorrow, though he never grows a day older than nineteen because Maya makes him a vampire by force.

By modern times, he is Thierry, Lord of Circle Daybreak, and Hannah is just a girl from Montana and this turns out to be the biggest Cinderella story of them all. Thierry seeks out Hannah during each of her lives–but Maya, mad with jealousy, makes certain that Hannah never lives to see her seventeenth birthday. Fortunately her last life is a little different.

As for remembering past lifetimes, Hannah has had so many that she really has to concentrate to find and then recall any particular one. But, yes, if she really works at it, she should be able to recall everything about each lifetime—all sixteen years of them.

Notes on the Chapters from L.J. Smith:
In Her Own Words

Hi, it's me again. I just wanted to make some comments about the various chapters in this book, and to mention things you won't find in the Night World series. How or why I wrote certain things in the books or what I think about them now. Little mysteries solved or hints of secrets.

Lamia

With the lamia, I deliberately broke most of the "traditional" vampire regulations. According to Wikipedia, "lamia" is just a word that in Greek mythology referred to a "child-eating daemon." I found the word in a thesaurus, and immediately began to use it in *Secret Vampire*. I wanted James Rasmussen, the lamia hero (*and* bad boy) of this story to be different from other vampires. No coffin for him! No all-blood diet! Not even a device to keep him from crumbling in the daylight like a traditional vampire, because these vampires aren't debilitated by sunshine! I also wanted to show that lamia parents can be just like human parents—rich and controlling parents, that is. Vampires live so long that they have plenty of time to get rich, and money leads to power.

One thing in *Secret Vampire* that gave me pause: Poppy North will forever be a teenager, and James would never continue aging without her. This means that they will be a sort of Peter Pan couple, with fangs. My take on this is that Poppy's twin, Phillip, will pity them as he gets older . . . until he reaches fortysomething and feels mortality creeping up on him. But by then it will be too late.

On the other hand, Phil probably wouldn't want to change.

I'm planning to write a short story about Poppy and James and Phillip for my website. I'd like to show what happens to the three wanderers when they reach Poppy and Phillip's father or show what happens to them when the apocalypse comes.

Final thought: I now wonder, why in the world did I create all these sets of twins or siblings who have similar names? I can only guess that it's because my sister and I grew up like twins, although our names (Judy and Lisa) don't show it.

Made Vampires

Made vampires are different from lamia in that they don't age and don't eat, but again I purposely broke most of the vampire traditions. One thing that was important to me was that the two groups of vampires form a unified front . . . of evil. Another was that even though lamia today believe they are the best kind of vampires, made vampires got some respect. Made vampires have no obligations to the vampire or lamia who changed them. Hunter Redfern, a lamia and the most powerful of all the wicked Night People (except for his ancestress Maya), was quite content to have a made vampire, Quinn, as his heir. In fact, he was adamant about it. But, for the most part, Quinn went his own way, especially as centuries passed. When Quinn obeyed Hunter Redfern, it was because even in the 1600s Hunter was the leader of the Night World Council (Vampire Division), and Quinn didn't care to be staked.

Making the vampires patriarchal (run by men) and the witches matriarchal (run by women) was fun. Especially since Thierry, who was raised a witch but made a vampire, revived Circle Daybreak. Thierry retained all his witch values throughout the millennia and deemed that the Circle would be matriarchal.

I got Thierry's first name from an "I love Thierry" graffito written on a bathroom stall! And I gave him my favorite last name, Descouedres. According to a Frenchwoman I asked, his name is pronounced "TEE-ry Day-coo-DRAY."

Ghouls

In order to write about ghouls, I had to read a book on death and the stages of decay of the body, and I will never forget it. It was incredibly morbid. It helped that I had already done some research on preserved mummies for my trilogy The Forbidden Game. Also, I was fascinated by a book about the Iceman, a remarkably well-preserved mummy found in a glacier in the Alps. Ötzi the Iceman died about 5,000 years ago and was encased in ice until a thaw revealed his head and neck and a hiking couple discovered him.

I feel very sorry for ghouls. They have no mental activity except what Terry Pratchett and *Resident Evil* both call "the need to feed." Their bodies keep decaying no matter what they eat. James Rasmussen's childhood nanny in *Secret Vampire* (Miss Emma), and even the ghoul Jez Redfern fights in *Huntress*, were innocent humans once, who didn't ask to become ghouls.

The kindest thing you can do for ghouls is treat them to a stake dinner.

Witches

Just like Mary-Lynnette, who became fascinated by the matriarchal witches while learning about the kinship ceremony in *Daughters of Darkness*, I also fell in love with this clan. From the beginning, Circle Twilight was a lot like Circle Daybreak, except that Circle Twilight witches scorned humans. I didn't write as much about Night World witches as I wanted because I had already done an entire trilogy about witches called The Secret Circle, in which I had used pretty much everything I could find or make up about Wicca.

The idea of witchlight grew slowly, and the importance of Hellewise and Maya grew too. I made family trees about them, the twin daughters of Hecate Witch-Queen, and the other first witches to leave a historical record of them. I had a very hard time giving their descendents names that sounded both a little like cave people and a little romantic. I ended up with rather silly names like Conlan Spearthrower (Thierry's brother, who mates with Hellewise.) Two I liked were Rushglow and Summer Ice.

Here's something that didn't get into *Spellbinder*: Thea is only a Harman by adoption. Her father was actually the Harman, and since witch names pass through the female line, she was born Thea Avery. Unlike Sylvia Weald in *Black Dawn*, though, Thea was never bitter about being born to a "second-class" family.

Shapeshifters

Although I mention shapeshifters in *Secret Vampire*, for a long time I wrote only about werewolves, if I remember correctly. And then in *Black Dawn* I made up shapeshifters who were also evil—and rather stupid. But then I was just sort of tackled by a shapeshifter who was everything that the previous shape-changers weren't. I'm talking about Keller.

Raksha Keller is one of those characters who just came to me, jumped me, and went on running, leaving me sort of stunned, trying to trace her by her tracks. I've always loved her, but I never knew what she might do next. If you want to know more about Keller and her soulmate, there's a story on my website called "Thicker than Water." She's also in *Strange Fate*. And between the two, there are some surprises, which, yes, I knew about from the beginning but couldn't get into *Witchlight* because of space.

The thing I like best about Keller is that she never pities herself—or at least she tries not to. And if she seems even more cold-blooded than Quinn, it's because she's a cat, basically, and anyone who loves cats knows how they value their independence. But Keller also has a completely pure and vulnerable heart, even if she herself doesn't realize it. She's like my cat Suzie, who was definitely not a lap cat and would jump into my lap and put her head under my arm, trying to hide there, when we went to the veterinarian.

Werewolves

I didn't mean to make werewolves so evil. It was wrong, and I don't know how it happened. I love wolves; I've read a lot about them. They are noble, playful, intelligent, and gentle creatures. But despite what I said about werewolves in *Daughters of Darkness*, that they were "wolves who sometimes looked like people," they acted more like wolf-dog mixtures. Hybrids can be unstable and just outright mean. I think that must be what distinguishes werewolves from the other shapeshifters, even from the Draches, who are the lineal descendents of *dragons*. Werewolves must have some wolf blood in them as well as some dog blood. That's what distinguishes them from noble wolves.

Of course, Lupe and other werewolves who join Circle Daybreak are undoubtedly descended from pure wolves. And, incidentally, gray wolves are considered either threatened or endangered in the United States, except in Alaska.

Maybe someday I'll be able to write something about the noble werewolves.

Dragons

Since there's a lot about dragons in *Strange Fate*, I'll mention here that just about every ancient people have legends about dragons, from the Aztecs to the Chinese to the Romans to the Persians to the Irish. Once you begin to look into it, it's almost scary. Really. The coincidences just keep piling up, and the more you research, the more you get a sort of strange sinking feeling. (Although, I'm a Virgo, so I'm very logical and don't believe in astrology or any of that stuff about Atlantis or ancient astronauts.)

Actually, the thing I find scariest about dragons is a dragon in human form. Just the thought of something that looks like a person but is actually a dragon, like the one Keller meets in *Witchlight*, with opaque black eyes and the soul of a monster—well, that gives me the shivers.

Humans, Vermin, Outsiders

The only thing I have to say about humans is that if you look around you, you'll find that a lot of things are still like the evil vampire system: designed to keep women in their place. If you don't believe me, try this: watch a commercial or movie or TV show and mentally change each character's sex. Just try it. Now, does it sound ridiculous when a boy runs away shrieking from an enemy while his honey grits her teeth and faces it? Do guys look cute with multicolored junk smeared on their lips and cheeks and eyelashes? Are they funny in miniskirts and high heels? Do you notice that on the news, male politicians, anchors, and correspondents are always smiling, while female ones are allowed to look grave? And that someone has decided that women are still very attractive when their hair is gray and they have some wrinkles, while men must always be young or at least have a face-lift every year? Isn't it odd that even the bravest boy needs a girl for *something* in the end?

I dare you to *really* try this a few times. Even on my own books, which were written to please editors. If you have a good imagination, you can do it easily. Don't just sniff and list a few books or shows where you think a strong girl or woman appeared. Try it today on *everything* you see. And then . . . whoops! Yes, that's the universe wobbling all around you.

Scarier than the Night World, isn't it?

Old Souls

I wanted to call *Soulmate* "Old Souls," but my editor at the time thought it would sound too . . . old. That young people wouldn't buy a book with "old" in the title. I also wanted the book to be much longer. Hannah (from Montana, and remember I wrote these books more than ten years ago) had so many lifetimes, and I wanted to show her in more of them. I wanted to show how Maya as a "friend" of her German teacher led young Viscountess Roshanna to a building that was bombed by the first Zeppelin raid in World War I. I wanted to show how, in ancient Persia, sixteen-year-old Anath was charmed by Maya into entering a cave full of serpents. And, of course, I wanted to show how Thierry tried, in each lifetime, to find and save his soulmate—but always failed. I researched those time periods and fell in love with them, learned all I could about each of them. I may still write the stories about them and post them on my website.

Hannah Snow, Lady Hannah of Circle Daybreak, is still very dear to me. She isn't just the heroine of the greatest Cinderella story in history (even *I* don't know how rich and powerful Lord Thierry is, both in the Night World and the human world), she's a worker who immediately began organizing things in Circle Daybreak. Old Souls don't usually dilly-dally, even though they know they literally have all the time in the world.

Of course Hannah has a large role in *Strange Fate*.

The Soulmate Principle

One of my favorite songs is from *Aida*. Not the old opera *Aida* by Giuseppe Verdi (although actually I love that, too), but the opening song of the rock musical by Sir Elton John and Sir Tim Rice. It's my favorite song in the whole musical, and the first two minutes and twenty seconds are really a ballad, which I digitally cut off just before the loud, dissonant chord.

It starts with the words "Every story, tale, or memoir . . ." and ends with "All are tales of love at heart." It's called "Every Story Is a Love Story." Try to find it sung by Sherie Scott. I'm listening to her sing it on Windows Media Player right now. (I put it on my computer before all my CDs were stolen at the airport.) This song holds me mesmerized and makes me cry.

Now that you've listened to it, you should understand the soulmate principle. It's a very, very old idea, much older than the original *Aida*. It comes from Plato, in ancient Greece, who may not have been serious about it. In the Night World most people aren't serious about it either—until it hits *them*.

The Prophecies

I wrote the *"One from . . ."* prophecy before I actually figured out how each line would be fulfilled. Of course, my editor at the time wanted to know how the four books I was proposing were going to work, so I had to figure out what each line meant. I wrote up four pages and completed the first three books easily. Little did I know that before I could properly start *Strange Fate* (*"One from the twilight to be one with the dark . . ."*) my life was going to change so radically that I would be left for ten years without the ability to write, even in my head.

There are actually three prophecies in *Huntress*. The other two are pretty self-explanatory. They were meant to be grim forebodings:

In blue fire, the final darkness is banished;
In blood, the final price is paid.

Four to stand between the light and the shadow,
Four of blue fire; power in their blood.
Born in the year of the blind Maiden's vision;
Four less one and darkness triumphs.

Circle Daybreak

Circle Daybreak was a tale that grew in the telling. I first mentioned it casually in *Spellbinder* because I thought it would be a good idea to have three circles of witches. As I've mentioned before, three is a very magical number. To balance Circle Twilight and Circle Midnight, there *needed* to be a Circle Daybreak.

I'd started the Night World series because I wanted to write stories of forbidden love. But after I'd gotten several illegal couples together, I realized that there ought to be some truly safe place to *put* them. And Circle Daybreak became the focus of all my hopes and ideals.

Although I have a very logical, pragmatic side, I also have a side that is pure idealist. And Circle Daybreak was born out of the desperate hope and belief that somehow, someday, everybody on this planet will be able to tolerate one another. That there won't be any more wars—between witches and vampires, or between countries, either.

By the time I decided it was Thierry Descouedres who'd revived Circle Daybreak, I knew that it had just about infinite money and influence behind it, and that it must have secret towns just as the vampires did. These secret Daybreak towns showed the best side of people, where my soulmates could live in peace.

Incidentally, Daybreakers still use their clan's flower to identify themselves, but many have changed the color to black and white petals alternating; to twin flowers, one in each color; or even to pure white. That's how the bad guys identify a Daybreaker.

The Wild Powers

Of the three Wild Powers who are already public, I like Jez Redfern best. Jez is another character who just sort of attacked me from behind, and her soulmate came right along with her, the way he does in *Huntress*. I've already written one long story about Jez and Morgead for my website, and I'll probably write more. Jez has endless stories to tell, and Morgead lives in a real building I used to visit.

Then there's Iliana. To fulfill the prophecy, I needed Iliana to be a Harman, with the traditional Harman features—but not exactly like Thea; more like her distant cousin Gillian. Keller was so responsible that Iliana *had* to be a complete bubblehead. I also wanted a triangle where all three sides were equally loving. Galen and Iliana made that easy: love just flowed endlessly out of both of them. Enough, even, to break down the barricade around Keller's heart.

Third, there is Delos. Mostly what I think about Delos is that he's used to being in charge, and that Jez is used to being in charge—and the time has come when they finally have to work together to hold off the apocalypse. Sparks are flying in *Strange Fate*, and it isn't just the soulmate principle at work.

And then there's the last line of the prophecy: *One from the twilight to be one with the dark. . . .*

DON'T MISS THIS
SPECIAL SNEAK PEEK AT THE
DRAMATIC CONCLUSION TO
L.J. SMITH'S
BESTSELLING NIGHT WORLD SERIES:

STRANGE FATE

Vampires, werewolves, witches, shapeshifters—they live among us without our knowledge. Night World is their secret society, a secret society with very strict rules. But the apocalypse is drawing near. And the Night World and the human world are about to collide in a cataclysmic way. . . .

CHAPTER 1
Sarah

Sarah wasn't trying to hear the whispering that was going on in front of her. She couldn't help it. Soft as it was, it seemed to override the teacher's voice.

"You're really getting me worried about homecoming. Are you going or not?" Rachel Carr was saying softly to Pamela Adams.

Sarah absentmindedly decorated math sums in her notebook with a design of flowers, which somehow seemed to make the voices even clearer.

"It all depends," Pamela answered, sighing. "The idea was to get Mal Harman to ask me, but so far . . ." She shrugged gracefully. "You know."

"Same with me," Rachel whispered back heavily, without turning to look at Sarah.

Sarah stopped drawing and stared at her notebook. Maybe they didn't know she was there. Since her mother's funeral a year ago, people often didn't know she was around until she spoke. And the two most popular girls at E. B. Turner High School didn't usually sit near Sarah or pay her much attention.

Rachel continued. "Don't worry, I'm not competing with you. I mean, I have my eye on Kierlan Drache. But the question is, can *either* of them be pried apart from that mousy little Sarah, even for one dance?"

The girls must not have noticed she was there. Pam and Rachel were always full of sweetness and light to Sarah in front of other people. But then, that was because Kierlan and Mal were usually the other people around Sarah. Sarah bit her lip. She would never last more than a few seconds in a debate with these girls, but . . .

No. She bit her lip harder, holding back the words, imagining herself in a cool green forest instead of this slightly stuffy first-period math class. Her teacher's droning voice became the creaking of the redwoods.

It was October 12 and no one had really asked her to homecoming, and she certainly hadn't asked anyone. But then, no one ever asked her to dances. What happened just happened by itself.

"So have you spoken to Mal about it yet?" Rachel asked Pamela. Somehow, despite how Sarah tried, the whispering, although soft, would not become the sound of leaves rustling in the trees.

"I'll make my move when I'm ready," Pamela said coolly, uncrossing and recrossing long, elegant legs in her very short white knit skirt.

"But it *is* Mal you're after—and not Kierlan, right?" Rachel demanded. Neither of the boys in question were in the honors math class. Mal was in regular math and Kierlan—well, he was supposed to be at the junior college for this class.

Pamela spoke indignantly. "Are you joking? As if I would even *think* about Kierlan after what he did to me last year at the Spring Fling!" Pam forgot to whisper as she tossed her glossy blond hair.

This got the two girls a long, stern look from Mr. Osford. Another student was called up to the blackboard, and Sarah hastily bent over and scribbled the exponential equation from the board into her notebook. Then she frowned, solved the problem, and decorated the numbers with twining vines. Much more elegant.

Math and art were the only two subjects that made sense to Sarah. She could never be a mathematician like Kierlan, but she hoped she could be an artist. In the big art room she had a painting hanging that had recently won a county prize, and she would be packing it up with Ms. Jessup to go to the state competition later that day.

But that doesn't give me long, gorgeous legs like a model's, she thought.

"No, no, no," Mr. Osford was saying to the student at the blackboard. "Like this, not like that."

Rachel and Pamela barely paused.

"Well, wear a long dress this time, then. He can't flip that." Rachel leaned over to pat Pamela's arm with a sympathetic air that held just a hint of smirk.

Pamela simply moved her arm and looked back haughtily. Pamela had everything a girl needed to look haughty, Sarah thought with sad admiration. She was tall, blue-eyed, a natural blonde, with a perfect, curvaceous figure and those long, long legs.

And Rachel was as perfect in her own way, with thick dark hair, wide dark eyes, and legs that were almost as elegant.

Sarah, on the other hand, was rather slight and fragile looking, with very little on top and nothing at all anywhere else. Coltish legs, no hips, flyaway brown hair . . . and a face that somehow couldn't do "haughty" at all, not that she tried.

"Anyway, good luck if you have to *ask* Mal yourself." Rachel whispered the words as if Pamela had proposed taking a swim in a river full of alligators. Sarah found herself nodding in agreement, then remembered she ought to want to skewer the girls and barbecue them for being so insensitive. Mal wouldn't barbecue Pam and Rachel, though, if Sarah told him about this conversation. Mal was the master of the cold stare.

"And that's supposed to mean?"

"Nothing," Rachel said hastily, in a placating voice. "It's just—there *have* been other girls who've tried, you know. They usually come back frozen solid. But at least if—*when* he says yes to you, you know you'll look great together."

And so they would, Sarah thought. No arguing with that. The gentle rustling of Sarah's green woods had retreated and Mr. Osford's voice grew louder, trying to make the power of exponents sound interesting with his inflection. Sarah very carefully drew a design of branching leaves around another sum.

"I just honestly can't see what they see in that Sarah girl," Pamela said in exasperation.

Neither can I, Sarah thought, suddenly breathless. She had to really blink to repress a sniff. She started worrying about what would happen when the class was over—would Pam or Rachel glance behind them when they walked out? If they did, it was going to be agonizingly embarrassing for all of them. And what about later? She had *art class* with Pamela, for pity's sake. How was Sarah supposed to act then?

Sarah moved ahead of Mr. Osford's lesson, copying questions from the board and solving them. She scribbled a gigantic Venus flytrap looming over the last equation.

Despite the hurt Sarah felt from Pam and Rachel's remarks, Sarah knew what was *really* going to happen. Kierlan, with his dark red hair, tawny eyes, and cheerful face, would definitely be the one to bring up the dance. He'd be sure to act as if they were all going to the dance together, if only as a joke. Everything was a joke to Kierlan. He'd ask when Sarah wanted to head off to "do-si-do" or "get down and boogie."

And then Mal would ask, coolly, if Kierlan had actually asked Sarah to the dance or if he was just making assumptions again. Sarah could almost *hear* Mal saying it. Mal was the opposite of Kierlan. Sleek, dark-haired, always perfectly dressed, with eyes that were like windows into the early morning sky, he'd definitely ask if Kierlan was making assumptions.

And then Kierlan would say that he and Sarah were too close for him to have to ask about every little dance. "So if *you're* planning to ask her," Kierlan would say to Mal, one arm casually thrown around Sarah's shoulders, "go right ahead."

And then both of them would look at Sarah for justification.

"You're not really going with this jerk?" Mal would say. "You know I've warned you about him. He's an animal."

And Kierlan would say, "But Sarah loves animals, don't you, Sarah?" Except, of course, that Kierlan almost never called her Sarah. He used the nickname he'd given her when she was five.

This nickname would both muddle Sarah's feelings and melt her heart. Then Sarah would look up helplessly at Mal, who would say that Kierlan was using undue influence, and that Sarah's decision should be entirely free of prejudice.

And somewhere in all this, the fact that Mal never—ever—actually asked Sarah to go with *him*, either, would get lost. And it would end the way it always did: with the three of them going together, the guys alternating turns buying Sarah flowers. And the three of them would spend most of the dance talking—and trying to keep Kierlan from slipping "a little something" into the punch bowl.

"So what color are you going to wear? Mal's not going to have much time if you wait around till the last minute," Rachel whispered, making it sound as if the deal was done, the arrangements already made.

Sarah thought of the lovely little homecoming dress that she had bought two weeks ago. It was aquamarine, to match her eyes, and she'd bought it knowing—assuming that she knew—exactly how the scene with Mal and Kierlan would play out.

Except . . . maybe things wouldn't happen the same way this year. Mal and Kierlan were seniors now; Sarah was only a junior. Maybe being a senior was more serious and things were going to be different this year.

The thought made her heart pound, and Sarah knew she couldn't stand much more of this. Class was almost over but—what if Pamela turned around? What if Pam realized she had overheard their entire conversation? What would Sarah *say*?

"I've got something in basic black; that ought to be easy to match," Pamela said. "What about you?"

"I bought something creamy—sort of ivory," Rachel said with a pat to her long dark hair. "Also easy to match."

Somehow that did it. That short exchange about the dresses, already bought and waiting—just like hers. Sarah suddenly heard someone speaking aloud, in a conversational voice, and then with a slight shock realized it was her own.

"Mal always wears black—but he doesn't like it on girls," Sarah said, watching Pam and Rachel start and turn to look at Sarah. "At least not since—," Sarah began, but discovered she couldn't finish her sentence. *At least not since my mother's funeral,* Sarah thought.

Now that Sarah was this far in, she turned to Rachel and said, just as loudly, "And if *you're* going to wear ivory around Kierlan, you're going to come home covered in punch."

There was a moment of perfect silence, and then Mr. Osford rapped sharply on his desk. "Pamela Adams, Rachel Carr!" he called. "Sarah . . . um, Strange! Are you three *looking* for a detention?"

Sarah, embarrassed as she was to find everyone in class looking in her direction, felt slightly vindicated.

Then, to her horror, she smelled roses. A shaft of pain shot through her head and she shut her eyes and pinched the bridge of her nose. Oh no! Not now! She *couldn't* have a migraine here.

Automatically, Sarah's other hand flew up. She lifted her head to see Mr. Osford shaking his head as if to say "give me a break." He looked to Rachel and Pamela, as if expecting their hands to go up too, but they sat stiffly, flushed, staring straight ahead like extras in a movie scene.

Sarah knew from experience that she was fighting the clock now. If she couldn't stop the migraine in the next minute or so, she wouldn't be able to hold it off at all. Without waiting for permission and with her vision already edged with sparkling silver, she stood up—and knocked her math book off her desk.

Sarah could hear scattered laughter, not really unkind laughter, but she didn't have the mental balance at the moment to judge fairly. All she knew was that she had to get out of this class.

Abandoning her books, trailing her backpack, Sarah hurried to the end of the row of desks. The pain in her head was coming more and more frequently, and she heard Mr. Osford say, "Sarah, I'm sure you can wait for the restroom for another six minutes."

Sarah was no longer paying attention. She lunged toward her goal: the door. Someone she couldn't see caught at her backpack as if to stop her. Sarah stumbled and there was more laughter. Mr. Osford, who had never had Sarah in a class before this year, asked, suddenly concerned, "Is something *wrong*?"

Someone else, far away, said, "She gets migraines."

Sarah found the doorknob by touch; the glittering silver aura now covered half her visual field. She opened the door and slipped through, just in time to hear Mr. Osford saying faintly, "Quiet down, everyone. A migraine is just a headache."

Not *my* migraines, Sarah thought grimly as she headed more by instinct than by sight through the empty halls toward the girls' restroom.

Not even Sarah's doctors could explain what happened when Sarah's migraines hit full force. They weren't classic migraines, but they weren't classic seizures, either. They didn't respond to medication.

All Sarah knew was that at the peak of the pain, she lost consciousness and had—nightmares. She had these same nightmares when she was asleep. But Sarah never told anyone about what happened in the nightmares, not even her kindly, sympathetic doctors.

Sarah was afraid that her kindly, sympathetic doctors would have her locked up.

Here was the girls' restroom. Thank God, she'd made it. She needed hot water. She stood at a sink and began running the water as hot as she could get it, ignoring the two senior girls who were putting on their makeup and talking.

Sarah leaned forward, breathing slowly and feeling the steam on her face. When the water was hot enough, she soaked a handful of paper towels and held them on the back of her neck. Sarah lost track of time. But she realized, gradually, gratefully, that the smell of roses had gone away, and that the shimmering silver covering her vision had retreated. She had caught the migraine early enough to stop it.

But she'd also left the hot water running in the sink. The entire mirror was misted over with steam.

Sarah realized that the older girls were looking at her pointedly. Hastily, she turned the hot water off and used her wad of paper towels to make a vignette in the misted mirror. She tried to shut out the glares of the senior girls as they scrubbed at their glass too.

Doing her best to appear casual, Sarah looked in the mirror. Her aquamarine eyes reflected back, their depths somehow giving the impression of being full of unshed tears.

The rest of her features were also all present and correct. Flushed skin that was usually pink, as she blushed easily. A small nose and a small, determined chin with a dimple. A nice mouth, if she thought so herself, and eyelashes that didn't require mascara. Hair: light brown and always falling in different configurations over her shoulders.

It was . . . a gentle face, Sarah thought as she turned away from the mirror. Sarah's mother had had a small, heart-shaped, gentle face, and Sarah took after her in that.

Sarah sighed, and turned to throw the paper towels into the garbage.

And was engulfed by the smell of roses.

CHAPTER 2
Wings

It happened all in an instant: the shaft of pain coursing through her head, holding her frozen again.

The smell of roses filled her nostrils, almost sickly sweet, much stronger than it had been in the classroom.

Sarah clutched feebly at a sink. Oh God, she thought wildly, this isn't fair! But her vision had already narrowed to a small circle, and she couldn't ignore the scent of warm, full-blown rose blossoms. They were so real she could almost see them. Sarah was going to have a migraine—right now—and somewhere down there was a very hard tiled floor.

She turned as another lance of agony shot through her head. Sarah was trying to get into a stall where there was privacy, when suddenly both of the senior girls screamed. The door had just burst open and a boy walked inside.

"This is the *girls'* restroom!" one of the seniors cried in outrage.

The boy answered indifferently, "Well, that's what I'm here to find: a girl."

The two seniors were still shrieking at him in fury and shock as Sarah tried to take a step forward. All she could see, in the center of her glimmering tunnel, was a tall boy with dark hair and chiseled features in a rather pale face. She saw eyes so light gray that they almost weren't a color, and two arms held out to catch her.

"Mal," Sarah heard herself whisper, and then, without question or hesitation, she let herself fall forward into the darkness.

And as she went, Sarah realized that today's migraine-nightmare was going to be a bad one. It started with wings.

Wings.

Crispy was squatting on her haunches at the far edge of the bone-yard. The white shape she had been staring at for the past few minutes was not some sheet of amazingly clean paper dumped from the Grand House. It was an animal. An animal with wings—a *bird*. She was proud of knowing that fact, and even more proud of knowing what kind of bird it was.

A pidge-un, Old Useless had told them when she described it. Not all things with wings were Masters, the old woman had explained to them. Not all things with wings meant death.

In the old days, Useless said, there had been lots of birds in the sky, the *blue* sky. That was before the Masters had purged the animals, of course, and darkened the sky, making it forever gray.

Despite her bragging rights, Crispy was deeply grateful that in the plump, gently curving shape of the pigeon, she could discern no sign of wings at all. Even knowing it was not a Master, she didn't think she could watch wings unfold without shrieking. And, considering the predators that lived in the boneyard, one shriek would mean her death.

Okay, so you've seen a bird. Now get back to work, said Crispy's mind, or, more accurately, said one half of Crispy's mind. It was the half that she privately called Smart Crispy, who knew what was *really* important and what wasn't. Important was surviving, gathering food, and most especially not getting caught and put back into the fawn pens where the little kids were kept to be fattened.

Important was not a bird.

Still, she sat. It's alive. It moves by itself, the other half of Crispy's mind marveled. This part was the part she labeled Dumb Crispy. Dumb Crispy was slow, but stubborn. What does it hurt if I sit here and watch the bird for a minute? it asked.

Crispy tried to remember other things Old Useless had told her about birds. Useless could tell you lots of things if she was in the mood; you just didn't want to get too close to her mumbling, toothless mouth. Useless'd lived her life in one of the crazies' pens, but somehow she had avoided the selections, and somehow she had escaped from the pen during the chaos of the Grand Hunt, the Hunt when Crispy had been burned. Old Useless'd cared for Crispy then. Now Crispy cared for her. A debt was a debt: that was an iron rule.

Besides, half the time Old Useless said that they were family. Sometimes she said she was Crispy's grandmother, sometimes her great-gran, and sometimes even her mother, a clear impossibility. It was probably all nonsense, but the thought that Crispy might really have a relative, even a crazy, white-haired useless old woman, made her feel warm.

And that's the kind of thought that gets you killed, Smart Crispy snapped. Can you imagine what Roach would say to that?

Dumb Crispy wasn't completely dumb. She was sampling the twilight constantly, instinctively. She was sniffing the air, opening her mouth so she could smell better, listening, glancing all around her, checking with all her senses for danger.

She hadn't reached the ripe old age of eight and a half by not paying attention.

Of course, she'd very nearly not reached that age. Crispy grinned, stretching some of the red scars on her cheek, and glanced down at her hands. One was full of graybread, the coarse, springy fungus that grew here and provided most of the food Crispy scavenged every day.

Her other hand was her baby hand. It was curled and stunted by the fire that had given her these scars, and it looked completely helpless. Old Useless was the one who had exercised Crispy's hand using herbs and poultices to take away the pain. Old Useless also claimed to be a witch and said she'd used the last of her witchlight to help Crispy, but Useless said so many different things that it was impossible to know what to believe.

However it was, by luck or chance or Old Useless's magic, Crispy had one good arm and one that *looked* withered but could do everything the other could. Like the two halves of her mind, the two halves of Crispy's body were divided, one normal, and one puckered with angry burn scars from her dusty towhead to her small, rag-bound feet.

Right now Smart Crispy was coming up with an idea that appalled Dumb Crispy. So you want to watch the pigeon? it said. Okay, I'll watch too. And I'll tell you something: there's *meat* on that bird's breast. Meat! Remember how long it's been since you tasted meat? *Can* you remember?

Dumb Crispy could feel her heart pound. The bird was harmless; it was free. It could get out of the valley, flying over the boneyard, over the hills that surrounded the Grand House and the farm that belonged to it.

She didn't want to kill it.

Then you'd better scavenge something better than fungus, Smart Crispy said. Because I know what Roach is going to say when she hears that you saw meat and didn't even take a shot.

All right, all *right*. Crispy blinked rapidly; she wasn't crying, of course— she never cried—but she had to blink before moving again. Slowly she stuffed the last cones of graybread into the rags that served her as a tunic. Then, slowly, reluctantly, she reached down to her rawhide belt, groping for her slingshot. It was makeshift, with almost all the materials gathered from the boneyard. A piece of tire from an old tractor for the cup. Bits of rubber for elastic and a Y-shaped metal pipe for a handle.

Then she positioned herself, inching upward, praying that the mound of garbage at her back wouldn't collapse. And all the while she *thought*. She thought herself part of the night, part of the boneyard, just another bit of garbage that a bird wouldn't notice.

At last Crispy was in line for a shot. Slowly she fitted a pebble into the slingshot. Now was the time to disappear into the boneyard background. The bird mustn't sense any danger. No danger . . . no danger . . .

That was the moment Crispy sensed the danger to *herself.* It was unmistakable, and it was *close.* It was just a hint over the reek of garbage, a rank odor that froze Crispy's heart.

Werewolf.

ABOUT THE AUTHOR

L.J. Smith is the *New York Times* bestselling author of the Night World series and the Vampire Diaries series. She has written more than twenty-five books for young adults, and she lives in the Bay Area of California, where she enjoys reading, hiking, and traveling. Her favorite place is a cabin in Point Reyes National Seashore. Visit her at ljanesmith.net, where she has lots of free stories for downloading.

Not all vampires are out for blood. . . .